He smiled and touched her hand. "You have a sweet soul, Helen Edwards. You always seem to see the good in people."

She blushed. "Thank you, Patrick. I'm afraid I'm not quite as good-hearted as you think. I struggle with ill thoughts toward people just as everyone does. It's a process, I guess. By God's grace, we grow in character."

"Yes, but some of us have prettier characters than others. I don't know anyone I'd rather spend time with." He touched her cheek. "There, I've embarrassed you. I didn't mean to do that."

"You didn't embarrass me." She turned her head. "Well, perhaps just a little. I enjoy your company, too."

"Helen."

Her pulse quickened as he looked deeply into her eyes. She caught her breath. She wasn't ready for this. Besides, nothing had changed. His life was in Atlanta. Hers was here. She jumped up. "I really need to check on Margaret. I'll see you at church in the morning."

Without giving him a chance to say anything more, she hurried inside.

FRANCES DEVINE

grew up in the great state of Texas, where she wrote her
first story at the age of nine. She moved to Southwest
Missouri more than twenty years ago and fell in love with
the hills, the fall colors, and Silver Dollar City. Frances
has always loved to read, especially cozy mysteries, and
considers herself blessed to have the opportunity to write
in her favorite genre. She is the mother of seven adult
children and has fourteen wonderful grandchildren.

Books by Frances Devine

HEARTSONG PRESENTS

The Scent of Magnolia

Frances Devine

Heartsong Presents

To my son, Jack, who hears and sees more
than anyone could imagine.
I love you, Jack.

A note from the Author:

*I love to hear from my readers! You may correspond with
me by writing:*

Frances Devine
Author Relations
P.O. Box 9048
Buffalo, NY 14240-9048

ISBN-13: 978-0-373-48638-0

THE SCENT OF MAGNOLIA

This edition issued by special arrangement with Barbour Publishing,
Inc., 1810 Barbour Drive, Uhrichsville, Ohio, U.S.A.

Chapter 1

Georgia, February 1892

Helen Edwards flung the gown, for she couldn't rightly call the ruffled, silk expanse of elegance a dress, into the growing pile on the floor of the cluttered third floor storage room. At least, it was a storage room now, whatever it might have been in the Quincy Family past. Bending, she pulled another sheet-wrapped gown from the ancient trunk, releasing a fragrance of spices and mothballs. Her breath caught in her throat as she shook out the lovely blue silk and held it in front of her.

She bit her lip as she gazed into the oval, French mirror that stood in the corner. If only her hair was blond or black or even red. Her brown locks pulled up in a severe bun, appeared mousy against the shining blue fabric. She sighed and focused on the dress. Should she try it on? How embarrassing if anyone should walk in and catch her, the proper, spinsterish school teacher, primping in who-knew-how-many-decades-old fancy clothing. She cocked an ear. Hammering and other noises from the west wing assured her that Albert and his helpers were busy with the third floor renovations. The Cecilia Quincy School for the Deaf would soon be moving their classrooms from the second floor of the old renovated mansion to the third with its much needed space.

Quickly she spread the gown across the trunk. Unbuttoning her sensible, dark brown, garment, Helen lifted it over her head and laid it across a straight-back chair.

A moment later, the sky-blue silk slid down her small frame. She closed her eyes for a moment and ran her hands across the smooth, billowing yards and yards of the skirt. Then taking a deep breath, she opened her eyes. Her breath caught. Why, she looked young. Nowhere near her thirty-two years.

A gasp from the doorway was the only warning that she wasn't alone.

"Oh! Miss Edwards. You're so beautiful. You look just like a princess."

Her cheeks blazing and heart thumping, she turned to the ten-year-old girl standing in the doorway, her blue eyes enormous.

"Please shut the door, Molly." She was careful to enunciate and look straight at Molly so the child could read her lips.

Molly Flannigan hastened to obey and then stepped over to Helen. Her hand reached out. She jerked it back. "May I touch it?"

Helen gave a nervous laugh. "Of course you may. Then I have to change back into my own dress before someone else comes in here. By the way, what are you doing up here?"

"Miss Wellington sent me to find you. She wants to talk to you about something."

"Very well. Would you like to help me put these things away? Then we'll go downstairs together."

Molly chattered in her slightly high voice and clipped off words as she helped return the garments to the huge trunk. She exclaimed over each one. "But who do they belong to?"

"I'm not sure. They're very old, so their owners must be long dead by now. I suppose they belong to Dr. Trent." Helen smiled, wondering what Dr. Trent Quincy's new bride, Abigail, would think of them. Helen couldn't wait to show her. It would be like Abigail to cut them all down into dresses for the little girls and fancy vests for the boys.

Helen wrapped the blue gown in its old white sheet and placed it on top of the others. Sighing, she closed the lid with a thunk then walked down the hall with Molly.

"I sure wish I knew who owned those dresses. They must have been awfully rich." Molly shook her head in emphasis, causing her long black braids to wave from side to side.

"I suppose they were," Helen said. "It's my understanding the school's original benefactress, who was our own Dr. Trent's grandmother, was quite wealthy."

"Is she the one who freed all her slaves?" Molly turned her eyes up to her teacher.

"That's right." Helen nodded and gave the girl's hand a gentle squeeze. "I'm pleased you remember the facts you've learned about the history of our school."

Molly's eyes danced. "Mrs. Alexandra Quincy, widow of Mr. George Quincy, freed all her slaves ten years before the Civil War began. She gave them all land and a cabin and the opportunity to work for wages if they wished. Soon afterward, she moved into a small house on her property and told her son, Thomas, to make the big house into a school in memory of her youngest daughter, Cecilia, who was deaf" —her expression sobered—"completely deaf like me. And they named it the Cecilia Quincy School for the Deaf."

"Excellent, Miss Flannigan. Perhaps you can recite those facts during the end of the year program."

"Really?" She giggled as they rounded the corner to the main hallway.

"Yes, really." Helen gave a gentle pull to one of Molly's braids.

"Miss Edwards?"

"Yes?"

"I won't tell anyone you tried on the dress."

Warmth rushed over Helen's cheeks. "Thank you. It would be rather embarrassing if anyone knew."

Molly nodded her head. "You want to know a secret?"

"Only if it's yours to tell and you want to."

"It is." She swallowed. "I used to try on Mama's dresses. You know, after she went to heaven."

Helen's heart lurched, and she paused at the head of the stairway, blinking back tears. "Oh, sweetheart. I understand. It must have made you feel close to her."

Molly swallowed again then nodded. "Pa walked in one day and saw me. He hugged me really tight. But when I went home again at the end of school, they were all gone. And so was her picture."

Helen put her hand on Molly's shoulder. "I'm sure your father thought that was best for you."

"I know. He said we had to move on. But we'd see Mama again some day." Her lips quivered. "Do you think that's true? Will I ever see my mama again?"

Gathering the girl into her arms, Helen sent a silent prayer for the right words.

"Your mother knew Jesus and so do you. Yes, I believe someday you'll see her again."

A sigh of relief escaped from Molly's lips. "I believe so, too. It's just sometimes it seems so long. And…I can't remember exactly what she looked like anymore."

The conversation remained with Helen as she went about her Saturday chores. She wondered if Molly's father knew what his daughter was going through inside. Probably not. He'd seemed distracted ever since his wife had passed away two years before.

Patrick Flannigan, with a grin he couldn't hold back, drove his buggy down the street toward home. He couldn't recall the name or the words to the tune he whistled, but its jolly rhythm matched the satisfaction he felt inside. Who would have thought his small leather shop would gain so much popularity. The last year he'd seen a steady increase, but in the past four months business had boomed. He'd need to hire more hands soon.

He stopped in front of the white frame house he'd called home since he and Maureen had married fifteen years ago. She'd have loved the improvements he'd made, especially the additions to the kitchen and the screened-in back porch.

But he knew, if she could see what was transpiring down here on earth, she'd be thrilled that he'd be bringing their little Molly back home soon. The school had been good for her. It had helped keep her from grieving too much. And she'd continued to learn things that would be helpful to her as she grew up. Her lip reading had improved and her speech was much better. He'd been tickled when she came home for Christmas and showed him the sign language she'd learned.

But it was time for her to come back home and live with him. Now that he could afford to hire more help he wouldn't have to work such long hours. And he could pay someone to care for her when he was away at work.

Hurrying inside, he picked up the clutter around the house then changed his clothes and packed a small bag. An hour later, he'd left his horse and buggy at the livery near the train station and was on the train headed out of Atlanta.

He sank onto a cushioned seat near the back of the car, grateful that the railroad now went through Mimosa Junction, a small town near Molly's school. Otherwise he'd be driving his buggy or a wagon all the way. Contentment washed over him at the anticipation of his little girl's joy when he told her the news.

Scuffling sounded through the room as the children entered and began to settle at their desks. Tommy Findlay pretended to trip and fell into his seat. A smattering of giggles greeted his comedic acting talent.

Helen, who stood next to her desk, decided to ignore Tommy's attempt to get attention.

"Boys and girls, please get settled and take out your history books."

All obeyed except Tommy, who hadn't been watching her lips. When he noticed everyone else, he hastened to remove his own book from his desk and look at the blackboard to find the page number. He darted a look at Helen, and relief washed over his face as he saw her indulgent smile.

When the books were opened, the children turned their attention to Helen's lips, waiting for further instruction.

"I'd like for you to read pages 102 through 107 and answer the questions on page 108. If you need help, please raise"—a knock on the door interrupted her—"your hand. You may begin now."

She stepped to the door and opened it to find one of the maids with her hand raised as if to knock again.

"Yes, Sally May?"

"Miz Wellington ast me to ast you to send Molly to her office right now." She gave a quick curtsy then added, "If you please, ma'am. I'm s'pose to walk with her."

"Very well, just a moment please."

Helen walked over to Molly's desk where the girl was already reading her assignment. She touched the girl on the shoulder.

"Yes, ma'am?" Curiosity filled Molly's eyes.

"Miss Wellington would like for you to come to her office, please. Sally May is here to escort you."

Molly's eyes widened. "Am I in trouble? I haven't done anything naughty, Miss Edwards. Truly, I haven't."

"Of course, you haven't. I'm sure it's nothing to worry about. Put your things away, please, and go with Sally May." Helen patted Molly on the shoulder and waited for her to get her things in order then walked her to the door.

Helen's eyes followed the two down the hall. When they started down the stairs, she shut the door and returned to her desk.

A little twinge of worry tickled at her as she went about her duties and helped the children who needed her. It wasn't like their director to call the child out from her studies. Helen only hoped there was nothing amiss. Molly didn't need another tragedy in her life.

Molly didn't return, but soon Sally May tapped on the door again, this time with a note from P. J. Wellington, informing Helen that Molly was spending the afternoon with her father and asking her to come to the office at the close of the school day.

When she dismissed the children at three, Helen slipped into her room for a moment to freshen up. She poured water into the washbowl and dabbed the cool liquid on her face. A glance in the mirror assured her all her brown curls were tamed and secured in the bun at the back of her head. She smoothed her skirt then walked downstairs to the director's office and tapped before opening the door.

P. J. Wellington stood at a window gazing out across the side yard. She turned when Helen entered. Her drawn face sent a wave of dread through Helen.

"Please have a seat, Helen." She sat in her chair behind the desk and sighed.

"You're frightening me, P.J. What in the world is wrong?" She frowned. "Not another death in the child's family?"

"No, no. Nothing like that. Although it may very well be the death of Molly's future."

Helen sat with her hands tightly clasped in her lap and waited.

P.J. slapped her hand on the desk. "Patrick Flannigan is removing Molly from the school."

"What?" Helen sat up straight. "But why? Does he have complaints about our curriculum or something else?"

"No." The fiftyish woman reached over and patted Helen's hand. "He had nothing but praise for Molly's training and education."

"Then why take her out?"

"It seems Mr. Flannigan's business has prospered and now that he can take care of his daughter's needs—including a nanny, it seems—he believes she should live at home with him." She gave Helen a sympathetic glance. "I know you've grown fond of Molly. I've only been here a few short months and I care about her. And she's thrived under your tutelage. But he seems to have his mind made up. I imagine he misses her and feels guilty for leaving her here as long as he has."

"But he visits often and she goes home during the summer and on holidays."

"I know. But apparently his mind is made up." She paused for a moment. "Perhaps you should try reasoning with him. After all, you've been Molly's teacher for more than two years."

"What is that, compared with being her father for nearly eleven?" She bit her lip. "Oh, P.J., Molly is such a bright child. And she's even shown an interest in teaching when she's older."

"Children often have dreams at her age that don't last."

"I know that. But at least she has dreams. I hate to see them dashed because of a lack of education." She sat up straight. "Where are they now?"

"He took her for a drive in his rented carriage. He promised to be back by supper time."

Helen stood. "Pray, P.J. Surely one of us can make him see reason. At least we have to try."

"I'll pray, but I'm afraid I've already said all that I can to the man. I'll have to leave any reasoning to you, my dear."

As Helen sat in the parlor and waited, she lifted her heart to God. There must be a way to make him understand how important education was to a deaf child. Surely he would see. She'd make him see.

"Now what are you pining about, Miss Helen?"

She raised her head to see Virgie, long-time retainer, who had been born into slavery but now ruled the household staff with iron tempered with the gentility of love.

"Oh, Virgie. Molly's father wants to take her home with him for good. How can I convince him he's wrong?"

Virgie eased her thin body down next to Helen on the settee. Her soft brown hand patted Helen's. "Have you asked the Lord?"

"Yes, I was praying before you got here."

"Did you ask Him the same thing you asked me?"

"Well, yes. Of course."

"What makes you so sure that's what's best for our Molly girl? Maybe the good Lord has a different plan. Maybe not. But you might ask Him what He wants instead of what you wants for that child."

Chapter 2

Where in the world were they? They'd been gone all afternoon. Helen paced her second-floor bedroom. Laughter floated up the stairs and in through her open bedroom door. She hurried out the door and glanced down the open staircase. Sissy, a young maid, had the newly hired Flora in tow. They disappeared down the first-floor hallway leading to the kitchen.

She turned to go back to her room but paused at the sound of carriage wheels. She stepped back out of sight and waited until the front door opened. Relief surged through her when Molly walked in followed by her smiling father.

Helen smoothed her skirt and patted her hair then started down the stairs. She arrived at the bottom just as Molly and Mr. Flannigan turned from hanging their coats on the coat rack.

"Miss Edwards!" Molly, with one braid loose and her black curls flying, hurried across to her and grabbed her hand. "We drove the carriage really fast. It was so much fun."

"That sounds like fun, Molly. Why don't you run upstairs and straighten your hair and clothing while I talk to your father."

"Can we take Papa up to the third floor and show him where the new classrooms are going to be?"

"If he'd like to see it, I'm certain we can."

"Oh no." Molly snapped her fingers. "I promised Lily Ann I'd help her with her arithmetic."

"Perhaps someone else wouldn't mind helping her," Helen suggested with a smile.

Molly's eyes brightened momentarily then her shoulders slumped. "No. I promised. Would you show Papa around while I help Lily Ann?"

"Now, Molly"—Mr. Flannigan gave an embarrassed laugh—"I'm sure Miss Edwards has things to do."

Helen hesitated. Perhaps this was her opportunity to speak to Molly's father uninterrupted. She threw him a brief smile. "Actually, I'm free until supper. I'd be happy to give you a tour of Quincy School's latest project."

"Thank you!" Molly threw her arms around her father's waist. "I'll see you in a little while." She hurried up the stairs.

Helen watched Mr. Flannigan as his eyes followed Molly. She could only call his expression adoring. There was no doubt in her mind that he loved Molly.

When he turned to look at her, his smile was almost boyish and his green eyes sparkled. Apparently, Molly got her deep blue eyes from her mother.

"Well, Mr. Flannigan, shall we go up, too?" Helen gave a nod toward the stairs.

"It would be my pleasure, ma'am." His smile broadened as he offered his arm.

The third floor was quiet for a change, except for the echoing sound of a hammer from the end of the west wing. Helen guided her guest to the double doors in front of them and they entered a large room with a stage on one end.

Mr. Flannigan whistled. "An auditorium, no doubt."

"Yes. Converted from the former ballroom." She motioned toward the stage. "This, of course, is an addition. Albert, our groundskeeper and stableman, designed it himself and built it with some hired labor and a lot of volunteers. We were totally amazed to discover he had all these talents. Well, Virgie wasn't surprised, but they've been friends all their lives."

"Will you be adding permanent seating?"

"No, Dr. Trent ordered chairs that can be easily removed if we wish to utilize the room for other purposes, such as parties or indoor activities on rainy days. They should arrive any day now.

They walked down the hall and turned onto the east wing. "Our younger children will be on this wing. She turned into the first room on the right. "This will be a combined play room and nap room for the five- through seven-year-olds. It was converted from part of the old nursery.

Helen showed him the classrooms on that hall, avoiding the storage room with the trunk full of ball gowns.

Mr. Flannigan nodded politely but didn't seem very interested. Perhaps the tour had been a mistake.

Helen hesitated when they arrived back at the stairway, uncertain whether to continue to the west wing. Suddenly she pressed her lips together and straightened her back. This was her opportunity to show Molly's father what he would be taking her from.

She continued walking. She turned into the west hallway, passed up the first room, and entered the second. The walls were filled with bright paintings, and tables and cases stood around the room, waiting for science projects and specimens.

"This will be Mr. Waverly's science class. Molly's favorite. She'll miss it very much."

He gave her a startled look then frowned but didn't say anything when Helen led him down the hall to the other rooms. His eyes brightened. "Molly is doing well with sign language, isn't she?"

Hope rose in Helen at his question. "Yes, she's doing very well. She shows so much promise. It would be a shame if she had to stop learning now."

Annoyance shadowed his eyes. "I appreciate your showing me around. When will you be moving the classrooms to this floor?"

"Very soon. Maybe as soon as next week." Although he hadn't replied to her comment about Molly leaving, Helen couldn't help the hope that remained in her heart.

But for now, she'd leave it alone. Perhaps she could talk to him after supper.

As they reached the second floor, Molly and eight-year-old Lily Ann came out of the girls' dormitory. The girls stopped in the doorway, signing into each other hands.

Mr. Flannigan's brow furrowed. "What are they doing?"

"Lily Ann has hearing, but she's completely blind. When we added sign language to the curriculum, she insisted on learning it, too. She signs to the deaf children, and they sign in her hand."

"That is amazing." He whispered the words, and Helen wasn't sure he intended them for her.

Molly noticed them standing at the stairs. "Oh, Lily Ann, it's my papa and Miss Edwards."

The girls hurried to join them.

"Papa, did you like our new schoolrooms? Aren't they

nice?" Molly grabbed her father's hand, and they walked down the stairs together. Helen and Lily Ann followed.

Molly didn't seem to know she was leaving the school. Had Patrick Flannigan not mentioned it yet? Was it possible his mind wasn't completely made up?

"Papa, is it all right if I play outside with Lily Ann until supper time?" Molly's long black lashes fluttered as she looked up at her father's lips.

"I suppose so. Perhaps Miss Edwards will consent to sit on the porch and visit with me while you girls play in the yard."

Helen threw him a surprised glance. She wasn't about to pass up the chance to talk to him more. She nodded and slipped through the door he held open. The screen door closed behind them, and Helen motioned to the wicker chairs and tables grouped at one end of the wide porch.

When they were seated, he turned to Helen. "I didn't realize you teach blind students, too."

"Well, officially, we haven't up till now." Helen glanced at the girls. "Lily Ann's parents are friends of Dr. Trent's. They didn't want to send her away to a school for the blind, so Dr. Trent agreed to take her as a student on a trial basis. She's been here two years now—since she was six—and learns quickly."

"But how do you teach her? Orally?" Amazement filled his voice.

"Yes, until recently that was our only method for teaching her. But we added braille to her course of studies a few months ago. She loves being able to read some of the simple stories for herself."

He shook his head. "You and your colleagues are doing wonderful things here."

"Thank you, Mr. Flannigan. We only do what we can

to make their lives better." *So please don't tie our hands where Molly is concerned.*

"Mr. Flannigan, would you consider changing your mind about taking Molly away?"

"You make me sound like some kind of ogre. Of course, I'm going to take her home with me. She's my child." He snapped the words then added in a softer tone, "I appreciate all you've done for Molly. Her time here has given her a chance at a much better life than she would have had otherwise."

"But don't you see? There's so much more for her to learn! Please don't cut her education short." Helen paused for breath. "Think about her future!"

"Her future is with her father!" He rose. "How can you think she's better off away from me? She's learned all she needs to."

"No, she hasn't." She noticed Molly glance that way and lowered her voice. "There is so much more for her to learn. Why can't you see that? Stop being so stubborn."

"Stubborn? Because I think my child belongs at home with me? This subject of conversation has ended, Miss Edwards." He turned and motioned to Molly.

"What, Papa?" Molly ran up the porch steps.

"Get your coat. You're coming with me."

Helen gasped. "But it's almost supper time."

His eyes were hard as they gazed into hers. "Miss Edwards, I'm quite capable of feeding my daughter."

Patrick tried to focus on Molly, who sat next to him in the carriage. But his thoughts kept going to that infuriating woman with her ridiculous ideas. How dare she treat him as though he were doing something evil when he was only trying to be a good father to Molly.

Why, she actually raised her voice to him. And those

eyes. Those strange blue eyes the shade of a spring sky that he'd thought so pretty had been clouded with anger when she shouted at him.

Well, he'd show her. He'd take good care of his daughter. Maybe he could find someone in Atlanta to teach her more of that sign language. He bit his lip. He didn't think that was likely.

"Papa, look." Molly pointed out the window at a dog chasing a black cat.

"Would you like to have a dog, Molly?" He patted her hand and waited for an excited reply. When she didn't answer, he realized she hadn't read his lips. He touched her shoulder to get her attention, and she looked up.

"Would you like a dog, Molly?" he repeated.

Her eyes lit up. "We have six dogs, Papa. We have a collie named Goldie, who lives in the barn. And she has five puppies. They're so cute."

He bit his lip and tried again. "Well, what about a kitten?"

"Oh, Papa. We have the cutest kittens. Nellie Sue, the mouser, just had seven of them." She giggled. "Virgie said not a mouse in the country would dare show its face around Quincy School."

He nodded. "That's very nice, Molly. I'm glad the school has pets."

He stopped the horse in front of the hotel. He lifted Molly down from the carriage and tossed the reins to the boy who stood waiting.

"Is this your hotel, Papa?"

"Yes, and it has a fine restaurant. I thought you might enjoy eating here tonight instead of the school."

"Sure. That'll be fun. I hope they have good things to eat like Cook does." She tossed him a big smile.

"Well, I'm sure they'll have almost anything you'd like."

He guided her to the restaurant door, where they were seated at a table set with crystal and silver.

They ordered fried chicken with mashed potatoes and gravy, sweet potatoes, and fried okra. Molly wrinkled her nose at the okra but ate the rest with pleasure.

"Well, what do you think? As good as Cook's?" Patrick eyed his daughter and grinned.

She took another bite of her drumstick and closed her eyes in thought. "Well, it's very good, Papa. And almost as good as Cook's. But don't tell her I said so. It might hurt her feelings."

Patrick laughed and made a buttoning motion on his lips.

Molly giggled. "You're funny, Papa."

They finished with chocolate cake and ice cream. Molly's eyes widened when she saw the enormous dessert in front of her.

After they'd eaten, they sat in the lobby and watched the people coming and going. They laughed behind their hands at a portly woman's wide-brimmed hat topped by a large blue bird.

"Papa, did you see my new classrooms?"

He hesitated. "Yes, I saw the classrooms. They look quite efficient."

"I know. Especially the science room. Mr. Waverly says we can go on more nature walks because we have more room to keep the insects and leaves."

Patrick watched her eyes grow bright with excitement as she talked about the anticipated new projects.

"You like your school, don't you?" Sadness ripped through him.

"Oh yes, Papa. It's the best school in the world. Did I tell you we have a new sign language teacher?"

"Yes, I believe you did. A Miss Wilson?"

"Yes, she's just out of college. And Virgie says if she's half as good a teacher as Miss Abigail was, she'll be wonderful." She paused to take a breath then giggled. "I mean Mrs. Quincy, 'cause she's not Miss Abigail any more."

She loved these people. He could see it in her eyes, hear it in her voice. But she was his child. She needed to live with him. That's what Maureen would want, wasn't it? He sighed. Maybe he needed to at least think about this before he did something he'd regret. He'd send a telegram to his assistant tomorrow and let him know he wouldn't be back as soon as he'd said he would.

Helen yanked the thread from the dress she was mending for the third time. She rethreaded the needle and tied a knot. Why had she spoken so rashly? What if she didn't even get a chance to say good-bye to Molly?

Forgive me, Father. Virgie was right. I didn't ask You what Your will is for Molly's life. I'm so sorry.

Helen started at the rattle of harness and the sound of carriage wheels. She waited until she heard Molly's voice and then the sound of her feet running up the stairs.

She rose and laid the dress on her chair then went to the foyer. Patrick Flannigan stood still, his face a myriad of emotions as he watched Molly fly up the stairs.

Helen cleared her throat, and he looked her way. "Mr. Flannigan, I spoke out of turn. Can you forgive me?"

"I will, if you'll forgive me. I wasn't very nice." He ran his hand around the band of his hat. "And perhaps you were right. At least you've given me something to think about. Good night, Miss Edwards."

"Good night, Mr. Flannigan." She closed the door behind him and started up the stairs, overcome with the goodness of God.

Chapter 3

The chalk screeched across the blackboard, sending a shiver down Helen's spine. She finished writing the homework assignment then turned to her class.

Her students sat with heads darting from the board to their tablets. Helen smiled at the diverse expressions on their faces—from Molly, who bit her lip as she concentrated with furrowed brow, to Sonny, whose bored expression and darting glances betrayed his restlessness.

One by one, they closed their tablets and raised their heads to look at her lips, waiting for instruction.

"Boys and girls, I know you're all excited about the chili supper at the church tomorrow night."

Phoebe Martin's hand shot up. The seven-year-old's eyes sparkled.

"Yes, Phoebe?"

"Do we get to help Miz Selma with the baking?" Hope filled her eyes.

"I think Cook said the older girls could help out this afternoon, Phoebe." Helen frowned at the giggles that rippled through the room.

"But, I'm seven." Phoebe's lips trembled. "Isn't that old enough?"

"Ordinarily, it is, Phoebe. You know Cook often lets you and Lily Ann help her. But today she needs the girls who are over ten and have been helping her a while." Helen smiled at the child. "But there will be other times when you can help."

The bell rang to signal the teachers it was time to dismiss. Helen's quick glance at the door alerted the other children, who looked expectantly at Helen.

"All right, boys and girls. As you know, there will be no classes this afternoon as some of the teachers and older students are helping with preparations for tomorrow. Be sure to do your homework. You may line up at the door."

Papers rattled and shoes scuffled against the hardwood floors as the children lined up at the door.

"Stop that!"

Helen jerked her head toward the line of students just in time to see thirteen-year-old Jeremiah jerk his hand back and stare at Helen. Sonny had grabbed onto the student in front of him to catch his balance.

"Jeremiah! Return to your desk." Helen gave him a severe look that broached no back talk.

"Boys and girls, you are dismissed." She gave a little wave then shut the door behind them and walked over to Jeremiah.

"We've had this discussion about picking on other students before, haven't we?" She tapped her hand on the edge of his desk.

"Yek mem." His broken, almost unintelligible speech aroused Helen's sympathy. Jeremiah had only enrolled at midterm and had very little training until he came to Quincy School. She straightened her back. She couldn't let her sympathy enable him to pick on the other children—especially the young ones like Donald and Sonny, who seemed to be his favorite targets.

He looked closely at her lips through narrowed eyes. Apparently he'd learned lip reading on his own and was very good at it.

"Jeremiah, I don't like punishment. But your mistreatment of the younger boys has to stop. I want you to clean the blackboard." She paused.

Relief washed over his face at what he apparently thought was his full punishment.

"I also would like for you to read Matthew 7:12 and write a half-page essay on what the verse means."

"A hak page?" Dismay filled his voice. "But..."

"No 'buts,' Jeremiah." She knew it would be a struggle for him because he could only print and still had trouble even with that, but it was necessary for him to learn not to bully.

"Yek ma'am." He rose and walked to the blackboard.

When he'd finished, Helen patted him on the shoulder. "Thank you, Jeremiah. Now hurry and get washed up for dinner. I hope you enjoy the chili supper tomorrow night."

A small grin tilted his mouth as left the classroom.

Helen gathered her things together and went to her room to freshen up. When she came downstairs, Dr. Trent stood in the foyer visiting with Mr. Flannigan. Molly held her father's hand with a look of delight on her face. The same look she'd had ever since he'd arrived.

She nodded a greeting.

"Helen. There you are." Dr. Trent smiled in her direction. "We were just about to go in to dinner. I can smell

Selma's good Georgia gumbo and I can't wait much longer."

"I agree completely," Helen said. "Will you and Abigail be at the chili supper tomorrow night?"

"Unless I have a medical emergency. I hear they'll be using Virgie's chili recipe and her spices."

Helen laughed. "Yes, Cook mixed up the secret spice mix yesterday, and Albert took it to Ezra Bines." When Virgie had stepped down as cook a few years ago to take over as head housekeeper, she'd given all her recipes to Selma, who'd been her assistant cook for years. Ezra traditionally made the community chili once a year in an enormous iron pot over a roaring outdoor wood fire. Although Virgie had given him her basic recipe, the spices remained a secret.

Mr. Flannigan held his free arm out to Helen. "Miss Edwards, may I escort you in to dinner?"

Heat warmed her cheek, but she placed her hand on the proffered arm.

Dr. Trent chuckled. "Well, all right. I know when I've been snubbed."

Molly dropped her father's arm and stepped over to the doctor. "You may escort me in, Dr. Trent."

The doctor bowed. "It would be my pleasure, Miss Flannigan."

Mr. Flannigan held Helen's chair then took a chair between P.J. and Howard Owens, the boys' dorm parent, at the other end of the table.

Helen smiled to see Dr. Trent at the head of the table. He wasn't here for meals often since his wedding. He gave thanks and asked the blessing on the food.

Sissy and the new server came in and began to dish up the soup. The smell of Georgia gumbo wafted across the room.

"Thank you, Sissy, it smells wonderful." Helen dipped her spoon into the savory stew. She'd had Louisiana-style gumbo before and loved it. Since coming to the school, she'd acquired a taste for the Georgia version. Chunks of okra, shrimp, crab, smoked sausage, and rice swam in a liquid of tomato sauce and delicious spices. The onion and various peppers tingled on the tongue.

The gumbo alone could have been a complete meal, in Helen's opinion, but before long, the servers removed the bowls and began filling their plates with tender pieces of steak in brown gravy, potatoes, and green beans.

When the meal had ended, Molly and two other girls helped to clear away the dishes. Helen smiled at their eagerness to help in the kitchen today.

Helen was in the foyer talking to Virgie when Mr. Flannigan walked out of the dining room.

He removed his hat from the rack and held it in his hands, running his fingers around the band. "Miss Edwards, I wonder if I might have a few words with you."

Helen tensed. Was this the moment he would tell her he had decided definitely to take Molly home?

Patrick stood beside Helen on the wide, white framed porch. He hesitated, uncertain what to do. "Would you like to sit over there?" He indicated the wicker chairs at the end of the porch.

"I think I'd prefer to walk down the lane, if you don't mind." Her smile was tremulous, and she motioned toward the gate.

"I don't mind at all." He offered his arm, but she didn't seem to notice. She gathered her shawl around her and walked down the steps.

"It's a nice day, isn't it?" Her hand waved, seemingly to the air in general.

"Yes. One of the reasons I love the South. Who would think early February could be so mild?" He glanced over. A soft brown curl had come loose and hung around her face. He wondered what it would be like to brush it back. He jerked his head around and looked forward just as she glanced his way. He didn't need to be having a thought like that about his daughter's teacher. They reached the gate and he opened it so she could pass though.

"So you're not from the South originally?" She waited while he closed the gate then continued down the lane.

"No, I grew up in Pennsylvania. I came to Atlanta to start a business with a friend." He realized he was still holding his hat and plopped it on his head. "He didn't care for Georgia, so after a year he sold me his share of the business and went back home."

"But you apparently like it here." She smiled.

"Love it. Still do." He paused then continued, "Besides, I'd met Maureen by then and didn't really care where I lived so long as she was with me."

Helen stopped beneath a live oak tree and looked into his eyes. "Maureen was your wife," she said softly.

"Yes." He swallowed past the sudden lump in his throat. "And that brings me to what I wish to talk to you about."

She stiffened for a moment then took a deep breath. "You're taking Molly from the school?"

"I'm still not sure." He shook his head, hating his seeming inability to make a decision. "Part of me thinks Maureen would want me to take our daughter home, but then I watch her with her teachers and the other children here. I see them conversing with sign language. She's happy here. When we went to dinner last night, all she could talk about was Miss Wilson, her new signing teacher, and how nice it would be when the school moves to the third floor.

She's happy because she gets to move from the dorm and share a room with one other girl."

"Yes, now that we'll have more room, only the small children will sleep in the dorm. The older ones are very excited."

"There's something else." Familiar pain and frustration gripped him. "Communication is difficult between Molly and me. Sometimes I forget to look directly at her when I speak or enunciate clearly."

Helen nodded. "Yes, I can see that would be a problem. You could learn to sign, you know."

Hope rose in him. That was the very thing that had been niggling at his mind. "Do you think I could?"

"Of course." Her blue eyes flashed with excitement. "Anyone can learn sign language."

Without thinking, he grabbed her hands. "Could you teach me?"

Pink washed over her cheeks, and he realized he was clutching both her hands. Quickly he released them. "Please forgive me, Miss Edwards. I meant no disrespect."

A gentle smile touched her lips. "I know you didn't and I'm not offended.

"Would you consider teaching me?"

"That would depend on how long you plan to be here, Mr. Flannigan." She bit her lip.

"I can only stay a week. I have to get back to my shop." He frowned. There was no way he could stay away longer.

"I can teach you some basic signs in that time," she said. "And we have a book you can take with you when you go."

"Wonderful! When can we begin?"

She held both hands up and looped her little fingers together. "This is the sign for 'friend.' "

Hopeful, but feeling a little foolish, he made the sign. "Is that right?"

Her lips tilted and her eyes sparkled. She leaned back against the tree. "Perfect." The smile faded. "Of course, Molly will be with you to help you learn when you go home."

Suddenly the solution came to him. At least a temporary one. "Miss Edwards, I think I should let Molly stay in school until the end of the term. In the meantime, I'll be learning sign language. Then I'll make a decision about next year."

Relief washed over her face. "I think that's a wonderful idea, Mr. Flannigan."

"I know you're busy, but could we get together for a short while every day until I leave? That way, maybe the book won't scare me to death."

A rippling laugh proceeded from her throat. "That won't be a problem. And since tomorrow is Saturday, would you prefer morning or afternoon for your lesson?"

"I promised Molly I'd take her to the river for a picnic tomorrow. Perhaps we could have the lesson afterward?"

"Of course." She pushed away from the tree. "And now I think I should get back and see if there's anything I can do to help Selma."

"Oh yes. The chili supper is tomorrow evening." Eagerness rose up in him. "Would you care to share a table with Molly and me?"

"I'd be delighted, Mr. Flannigan," she said. "Perhaps Molly and I can teach you some signs for the food and utensils."

"In that case, Teacher, perhaps you could drop the mister and call me Patrick."

A startled look came on her face. "I suppose that would be all right." She lifted her chin. "And you may call me Helen."

Helen sat in front of P.J.'s desk. "Patrick Flannigan has decided to leave Molly here until the end of the term."

"Ha!" P.J.'s eyes shone. "I knew you'd get to him."

"What do you mean?" Helen hoped her voice was as shocked as she felt. "Why, I had nothing to do with it. He decided on his own."

"Uh huh." P.J. grinned. "I'm only teasing, Helen. Don't get all riled up."

"Well, that wasn't nice, P.J." Helen bit her lip. Their director needed to grow up, even if she was fifty years old. "Apparently, it's obvious to him that Molly loves it here. He also realized he needs to learn sign language so they can communicate better."

"Bravo for him. He's a father who puts his child first. That's refreshing." P.J. frowned. "But why did he plan to take her out of school in the first place?"

Helen hesitated. "I believe he thought his late wife would want him to bring their child home."

"Hmmm." P.J. tapped a pencil against her desk. "How long ago did his wife pass away?"

"It's been a little over two years. Molly still grieves for her mother sometimes."

P.J. nodded. "I've often found that after a while the memory starts to fade and people feel a little guilty. So they put restrictions on themselves that their loved one would have never wanted."

"You could be right," Helen said. "Molly told me she can't always remember what her mother looked like. Mr. Flannigan may be going through something similar."

"So what is the plan? Do we give him a book to take home with him?"

"Yes. And I've agreed to teach him a few basics before he leaves next week."

Amusement crossed P.J.'s face. "You? Why not the sign language teacher?"

Helen gasped. "Oh dear. When he asked me to teach him, it never crossed my mind to suggest Hannah."

"Oh well, she has enough right now anyway, learning the school and getting used to all the children. Perhaps it is best for you to do it, if you don't mind." She grinned.

"Stop looking at me like that." Helen stood. "I'm only trying to be helpful. For Molly's sake. I have to go see if Cook needs my help in the kitchen."

P.J.'s laughter followed Helen down the hall.

Chapter 4

Children's laughter rang out across the schoolyard. Games of tag and hide-and-seek were already in full swing. The late afternoon sun cast shadows, and although it was a warm day, Helen, who sat on the top step of the church, shivered when a gust of air passed over her skin.

"Mmm, that chili smells wonderful." At the sound of Abigail's cheerful voice, Helen turned.

"It sure does. You missed the chili supper last year, didn't you?" Helen looked up from the step at her friend.

Abigail laughed. "Yes, by a good while. I can hardly believe it's only been eight months since I arrived here." She gathered her skirts around her and settled next to Helen.

"You know we're going to be right in the way of folks going in and out of the building." Helen made the observation but made no move to rise.

"I know, but it's the perfect spot to see everything."

Abigail wrapped her shawl across her stomach, leaving her hand there for a moment.

Something about the protective movement sent a rush of excitement through Helen. "Abigail! Are you expecting?" Her excitement was reflected in her whispered words.

"Shhh. Yes. How did you know? Am I showing?"

"No, silly. You can't be more than a couple of months along. It was the way you laid your hand over your stomach." She noticed the redness cross her friend's cheeks and felt warmth in her own. "Forgive me, Abigail. I shouldn't have been so outspoken."

Abigail giggled and flicked her wrist at Helen. "Oh, it's all right. But I'd better be careful or the whole community will know before I tell Trent."

Helen gasped. "Oh my. You haven't told him yet?"

"I wanted to wait a while to make sure." She cut her glance at Helen.

"But you are sure, aren't you?" Helen grinned.

"Yes. I'm going to tell him tonight." Abigail gave a little shake of her finger in Helen's direction. "Don't you dare say anything. He has to think he's the first to know."

"I promise." She stood and held her hand out. "You'd best get up from there. Let's go inside."

Abigail waved her hand away. "Don't coddle me. People will notice."

"All right. Let's see if we can bring the silverware out to the tables." Helen stepped up onto the porch, keeping an eye on her friend."

Baskets of desserts and breads sat on a table at the back of the church. Odds and ends of forks, spoons, and knives, donated by the ladies of the community from time to time, lay in a bucket waiting to be taken outside.

Virgie and Selma stood giving directions.

Helen laid a hand on Virgie's wrinkled brown arm.

"What can we do to help? Is the silverware ready to go out?"

"Yes, but grab that stack of tablecloths to put over the tables. Them boys been scrubbing them down, but I don't want to take a chance they missed a spot of bird droppings."

Helen heard something like a cough or gag from behind her. She grabbed the tablecloths and shoved them into Abigail's hands. "I'll be right behind you with the utensils."

She grabbed the bucket and followed Abigail outside and down the steps.

Abigail bent over, making choking sounds.

Helen put her arm around her. "Honey, are you all right? Should I get Trent?"

Abigail stood up straight and looked at Helen, her face contorted, then emitted a loud guffaw.

Helen stepped back. "You're laughing. I though you were nauseated because of what Virgie said."

Abigail grabbed Helen's arm to steady herself. "I'm sorry. I couldn't help it. The thought of covering up bird droppings with Virgie's spotless white tablecloths was too much."

Laughter bubbled up in Helen and exploded. She linked arms with Abigail and they walked over to the line of tables, still laughing.

"Well, ladies, are you going to share the joke?"

Helen gasped and looked up to see Patrick walking toward them, a smile on his face.

"Oh, Mr. Flannigan. It was nothing." Helen took a deep breath to regain control. "But please come meet my friend Abigail, Dr. Trent's wife."

Abigail offered her hand, and Patrick took it and gave a gentle shake. "I'm very pleased to meet you, Mrs. Quincy."

"And I'm delighted to meet our sweet Molly's father

at last." Abigail looked from Patrick back to Helen. "I'd better get these cloths on the tables so we can get the dessert table set up."

She began shaking out the cloths and smoothing them down on the long board tables.

Helen darted a glance at Patrick and found him giving her a very admiring look. She blushed. "If you'll excuse me, Patrick, I need to help Abigail."

"Of course. I'll just go see if I can help stir chili or something." He grinned.

"Ezra will run you off if you come near his chili. But I think I saw Dr. Trent getting the boys together for a game of kickball." She glanced toward the back of the church. "Yes, there they are. He could probably use another man to help keep order."

"I'm your man. I'll go see what I can do." A red lock fell across his forehead, nearly reaching his eye.

She'd never noticed how handsome he was before. Well, maybe she had, at that. She watched him walk away.

"Come on, Miss Lovelorn. I could use some help here." Abigail's laughter rang out again.

Humph. Abigail had been laughing a lot lately. She must really like married life. But why did she have the idea Helen was lovelorn? She felt herself blushing again. It seemed she was blushing as much as Abigail was laughing.

She turned and grabbed an end of the cloth Abigail was trying to get onto the table evenly. "I'm not lovelorn. Don't be silly."

"You don't like Mr. Flannigan?"

"Well, yes, I like him. He's a very nice man. But not the way you are implying." She blew a lock of hair out of her eyes and frowned at her friend. "The very idea. I hardly know him."

Contrition crossed Abigail's face. "Forgive me, Helen.

I shouldn't be teasing you. I remember how I felt when people would tease me about Trent. Before I even knew I loved him."

Helen gave her friend a suspicious look. "Well, don't think I'm in love with Patrick Flannigan. Because I'm not."

"Oh no. I was only talking about me. And Trent." Abigail bit her lip then cleared her throat. "We'd best get the rest of the cloths on the tables. I see some ladies coming with baskets of food."

"Yes, and from the way the chili smells, I'd say that it's almost ready, too." Helen helped smooth the last cloth just in time. She and Abigail helped get the bowls and plates set up on one end of the table. They laid out spoons, forks, and knives in separate piles. Soon the breads and desserts covered one of the tables. And little bowls with chopped onions and chopped peppers were placed around the tables.

Reverend Shepherd stood on a tree stump and called out for everyone to hear. "Let's gather around now and say grace, brothers and sisters. The crowd flocked around, and after thanks had been given, they lined up with their bowls.

Patrick appeared at Helen's side. "Molly is saving three seats at the second table. We already have our chili and corn bread and she sent me to fetch you."

Patrick couldn't remember the last time he'd enjoyed himself so much. From the delicious food to Molly's giggles when he made a mistake signing the word for one of the utensils. Helen's delight when he got them right made him work harder just so he could see her eyes sparkle and her soft pink-tinged lips tip into a smile.

"Papa!" Molly tugged on his sleeve. "Why are you staring at Miss Edwards?"

"Uh…" He laughed. "Well, she's a mighty pretty lady, don't you think?"

"Oh, Papa, 'course she's pretty."

Helen's face flamed. "Well, thank you both, but could we talk about something besides my appearance?"

What had he been thinking? That was the problem. He hadn't been thinking. "I'm sorry, Helen. It just sort of blurted out. I didn't mean to embarrass you."

"That's quite all right. I realize you were being polite." Her face still flushed, but at least it wasn't beet red anymore.

"Okay, Molly, you didn't show me the sign for knife." He hoped Molly would follow his lead and change the subject.

The men brought out lanterns, hanging them in the trees and standing them on the tables and the porch as dusk started to fall.

Some of the younger children were nodding off to sleep, so their mothers began to gather up platters and leftovers to take home.

Helen rose. "I need to help clear away."

"Will you ride with us, Miss Edwards?" Molly pleaded.

"Well…"

"I was about to invite you myself." And he regretted that Molly had beaten him to it. He enjoyed Helen's company and wasn't quite sure why. Of course, she was a very kind and gentle woman and was obviously Molly's favorite teacher. So naturally, he liked being around her.

"That was so much fun, wasn't it, Papa? And that chili was as good as Cook's. Didn't you think so, Miss Edwards?" Molly continued to chatter practically nonstop on the ride back to school.

Patrick grinned. He suspected his daughter was talking to stay awake. "I'll take you to the hotel for lunch tomorrow, Molly girl. How does that sound?"

"Fried chicken?" She leaned her head on his shoulder and patted a yawn.

"Fried chicken it is." He glanced down, but her eyes had closed. He glanced over at Helen and smiled.

"I think she's off to dreamland," Helen said. "She's had a busy day."

"Thank you for spending your time with us tonight. It meant a lot to Molly." The reins hung loosely in his hands, and he let the horses go at their own pace.

"It was my pleasure. She's very dear to me."

"To be honest, it meant a lot to me, as well." He cleared his throat. "I haven't had the pleasure of a lady's company very much since my wife passed away. I'd forgotten how nice it was."

She was silent and he could have kicked himself. He seemed to be speaking out of turn a lot lately.

"Thank you, Patrick. I enjoyed the evening, too." She patted back a yawn. "Oh, excuse me. It must be catching."

He laughed. "Nothing to excuse. I'm a little drowsy myself. So are you still willing to give me a sign language lesson tomorrow afternoon?"

"Yes, of course. And Miss Wilson has put some things together for you to take home with you when you go. A sign language book and a book about life for the deaf. She thought it might help you when you take Molly home."

"That's very kind of her. I'll be sure to thank her." He turned into the dark tree-lined lane leading to the school.

Helen was silent, and he glanced over to see if she'd joined Molly in her slumber land. A moonbeam made its way through the branches and bathed her hair and skin with pale gold. His breath caught in his throat and she looked up at him with a question in her eyes. "Did you say something?"

"No, no. Just a hiccup." Well, that was brilliant. What

in the world was wrong with him tonight? He'd allowed moonlight to affect his brain.

He stopped the carriage at the front porch. He came around and helped Helen out of the carriage then lifted a groggy Molly down.

Helen put an arm around her. "Why don't you let me take her inside and help her get to bed."

"If you're sure." He bent over and kissed Molly on the cheek then looked at Helen. "I'll be here to get Molly around eleven in the morning."

"I'll make sure she's ready."

"Good night, Papa." Molly yawned then leaned against Helen as they walked up the porch steps.

Patrick watched them go. A strange longing shot through him and his eyes misted. Spinning on his heels, he got back into the carriage and drove down the lane.

Helen took Molly to her dorm and left her in the girl's dorm mother Felicity's tender care, even though what she really wanted to do was tuck the child into bed and sit by her side until she went back to sleep. She'd been warned all through her training to care about her charges but not get attached. How did one not get attached to a child?

All right, she had to admit she wasn't as close to the other students as she was to Molly. There had been a special bond between them from the day Molly had arrived. Her heart had gone out to the little girl who had so recently lost her mother. But as time went on, her attachment to Molly had nothing to do with sympathy over the girl's grief. She loved the child for herself. And she should have guarded against that. Guarded her own heart and Molly's, too.

She couldn't fool herself. Patrick loved Molly and missed her. That was obvious. And although he'd been wise enough to see he wasn't ready to take her with him, Helen knew he would do whatever was necessary to get ready. He would have his daughter with him and soon.

With a need to escape her own thoughts, Helen went downstairs in search of someone or something to distract her. She heard voices in the parlor and relief washed over her.

Virgie and P.J. sat with cups of steaming tea. Suddenly there was nothing Helen wanted more than a cup of tea.

She sank into one of the overstuffed chairs. "Is there anything left in the pot?"

"Half full and still piping hot." Virgie reached for the extra cup and saucer on the tray." Thought you'd be needing this when you got here."

"Thanks, Virgie. You're an angel."

Virgie chuckled. "I'm no such thing. The good Lord created angels and the good Lord created people. Take another look."

Helen couldn't help the giggle that came up from deep inside. "Oh Virgie, what would I do without you? You're a breath of joy."

Virgie handed over the steaming cup. " 'The joy of the Lord is your strength.' Just like the good book say it is."

Helen let Virgie's soft, soothing voice wash over her.

P.J. sat straight up and stared at Helen. "What's wrong with you, Helen?"

"I'm just tired. It's been a long day." She took a sip from her cup and let the hot liquid flow down her throat.

P.J. frowned. "Today has had the same length of time as any other day. Maybe it was just a little more filled up than most."

Helen leaned back and listened to P.J. talk about moving the classrooms up to the third floor in two weeks. She tried to let the words push out the thoughts of Molly and

Patrick. But the thought that came to her in response to P.J.'s words was that Patrick would be gone the following weekend. And Helen didn't like the thought at all.

Chapter 5

Patrick watched the screen door shut behind Helen. She had said her farewell and left him and Molly to say good-bye in private. He hoped Helen hadn't gone far. Molly would need her teacher's comfort when he drove away.

He lifted his daughter's chin and mouthed the words *I love you*. Then he made the sign for it, and Molly's mouth dropped open.

"Papa! When did you learn that?" Molly's deep blue eyes sparkled with excitement mixed with her tears.

"Miss Edwards taught me yesterday." He smiled and flicked Molly's braid. "She thought we might need it."

"Oh, Papa." Molly flung her arms around his waist and squeezed. "I wish you didn't have to leave."

A twinge of sadness shot through him that she hadn't said *I wish I could go with you*. Apparently, it hadn't even crossed her mind that she might. He sighed. He was glad he'd never mentioned his earlier intentions to her.

"I'll be back next month," he reminded her.

"You promise?" She stared up into his face.

"I do." In fact he might not wait a month, but he didn't wish to build her hopes up until he knew he could get away from the shop sooner.

She nodded. "All right, Papa. But you'll write me letters?"

"I will. In fact, I'll write to you on the train and mail it when I get to Atlanta." He stroked her hair back, glad it hung loose today. She had the same black curls and deep blue eyes as her mother.

"And you'll tell me all about the train ride?" Her lips trembled, but she pressed them together and held her chin up.

"Every single thing. I'll even eat in the dining car so I can tell you about the food." He grinned.

"There's a dining room on the train?" Her voice rose with incredulity.

"There sure is. I saw a little girl eating one of those new ice cream cones I told you about."

"You sure you aren't making that up just to tease me? Do they really serve ice cream in cones made out of cookies?"

"Well, not exactly cookies but something similar. I'll take you to the candy store in Atlanta this summer and prove it to you." Anything to get those tears from her eyes.

She nodded and rubbed the toe of her shoe against the ground. "Summer's a long time away." Her mournful tone stabbed at his heart.

"Not really so very long, sweetheart. Time will pass quickly for you with all the excitement of moving the school's classrooms. And don't forget you'll have a new bedroom soon and just one girl to share it with."

A sigh escaped her lips, but she nodded. He could still hear the sigh when he drove down the lane and headed for Mimosa Junction.

Helen awoke to a sunshiny Saturday. She yawned and stretched lazily then glanced at the little clock on her bedside table. Six thirty! She needed to hurry or she wouldn't have time before breakfast for her morning devotions. And heaven only knew if she'd have time later in the day; she'd be so busy helping with the move. After hastily washing up, she dressed then picked up her Bible and sat in the rocking chair by her window.

A cardinal flew past the window with a flash of red that reminded her of Patrick's curls. He'd been gone nearly two weeks and she couldn't believe how much she missed him. With a guilty start, she opened her Bible. *Forgive me, Lord, for letting a foolish thought keep me from Your Word.*

She had finished 2 Timothy yesterday, so she opened to the first chapter of Titus and began reading Paul's instructions concerning the appointment of bishops. She gasped when she came to verse six.

Of course, the rule about only one wife referred to a monogamous relationship and Maureen was no longer living. Still, it appeared Patrick was still very much in love with his deceased wife. One more reason for Helen to banish any stray thoughts of romance from her mind. Even if she cared for him in that way—which she certainly didn't—he would never see her as more than Molly's teacher or even a friend.

A sudden sound of shuffling feet and muffled giggles startled her from her thoughts. Oh no. It was time for breakfast and she'd not finished her Bible reading. With another quick apology to God, she arose, smoothed her skirt then followed the children and their dorm parents downstairs.

P.J. was practically bouncing as she came from her downstairs apartment. "Helen! This is the day."

Helen laughed. "Yes, it is. And I suppose everyone is here and ready to get busy."

"Well, no. But I told them all to eat a good breakfast first. Dr. Quincy and Abigail won't arrive until midmorning as he had a patient to visit first." She linked her arm through Helen's and they walked into the dining room together.

The children were almost too excited to eat and had to be reminded several times to settle down. By the time the meal was over, several volunteers had arrived to begin moving furniture. Felicity and Howard sent the children outside to play. The two neighbor girls who volunteered from time to time promised to keep a close eye on them while the adults worked.

Helen had already packed up most of her classroom books and supplies but headed to the second floor after breakfast to finish up. She went into Abigail's classroom, which hadn't been in use since last semester. She smiled as she walked over to the small table and chair near Abigail's desk where Lily Ann had sat and worked while Abigail taught the deaf children English and spelling. After Abigail's wedding, Lily Ann's braille instructions had stopped temporarily. Helen and Charles Waverly, the science teacher, were learning the written language for the blind. In the meantime, they both taught the child orally as they had before braille had been added to the curriculum.

Abigail had planned to teach the little girl for a while after her honeymoon, but now with the baby on the way that wasn't likely. Helen sighed. Abigail had allowed herself to become attached to Lily Ann just as Helen had to

Molly. It made things more difficult when circumstances changed. Should she pull back a little from Molly? A knot formed in her stomach, and she shook her head. Not yet. If Patrick really did remove Molly from the school, she'd just have to cross that bridge when she came to it.

A sound of laughter drew her attention to the window. Stepping over, she looked out over the yard and saw Albert driving Dr. Trent's carriage into the barn. Oh good. Abigail was here.

Quickly, she finished packing the last box then went downstairs and into the parlor.

Abigail looked up and set her teacup on the table beside her chair. "Helen! This is so exciting. Come have a cup of tea with me and tell me what I can do."

"Just talk to me for a while. We haven't had a chance to visit since the chili supper." Helen leaned over and gave her friend a hug.

"But surely I can help pack up school supplies or something." She frowned.

Helen laughed. "Sorry. Too late. I'm all done. And so are the other teachers." She sat on the settee by Abigail and accepted a cup of tea. "Don't worry. There will be plenty to do next Saturday when we move the children into their different rooms."

"What happens to the dormitories?" Abigail took a sip of tea and then threw Helen a questioning look.

"They plan to convert the girls' dormitory into a bedroom and sitting room for Felicity. I believe Howard has chosen to have one large bedroom with a corner for a desk, so the boys' dorm will be converted into a large bedroom for him and a small utility room."

Abigail nodded. "And the former classrooms will be converted into bedrooms for the students."

"Yes, and they are so excited." Helen put her cup down on the table and leaned back.

Abigail sighed. "I'd wanted to explore the third floor before they started remodeling, but I missed my chance."

Helen sat up. She'd almost forgotten. "Abigail, you'll never believe what I found in one of the storage rooms."

Abigail's eyes filled with curiosity. "Well, tell me, please. Not a dead rat or something else nasty, I hope."

"Ewww, no." Helen cringed. "I wouldn't be sharing that with you. I found an old trunk full of absolutely gorgeous ball gowns."

"Where in the world did they come from?"

"They're very old. I would say they've been there since before the War." Helen picked up her cup and took another sip.

"Really! They must have belonged to Trent's grandmother and aunts." Abigail's eyes brightened. "What shape are they in?"

"That's the surprising part. They were wrapped in sheets and seemed in fairly good shape."

"Hmm. They'd probably fall apart if anyone tried to put them on," Abigail said.

Helen squirmed for a minute then cleared her throat. "Well, actually, I tried one on." She grinned. "It held up quite well. I think they might be useful for making costumes."

"You mean for the end of school program?"

"Why not?" Helen shrugged. "Perhaps we could write a play based on those old days."

Abigail gasped. "We could have a reenactment of Mrs. Quincy's freeing of the slaves and the beginning of the school."

Helen nodded. "My thoughts exactly."

"Is the trunk still there?" Abigail jumped up. "Let's go look."

"I have a better idea," Helen said. "Why don't we ask a couple of the men to bring the trunk down here? That way you won't need to climb all those stairs."

Abigail heaved an irritated breath. "Please don't treat me like an invalid."

"I wouldn't dream of it." Helen chuckled and pulled her friend down beside her with a gentle tug on her arm. "But there are a lot of things up there you could trip over today."

"You're right." Abigail folded both hands on her stomach for just a moment. The expression on her face was one of wonder and awe. She let her hands slide onto her lap. "I'd never forgive myself if my baby came to harm because of my carelessness."

After lunch, Albert and one of the neighbor men brought the trunk down to the parlor. Helen motioned to Virgie, who was walking by the door.

"What you bring that old trunk down here for?" Her soft voice nevertheless held a hint of disapproval when she saw the bound luggage sitting in the middle of the parlor floor.

"It's full of fancy dresses." Helen lifted the hasp and opened the lid. "Do you recognize these?"

The old woman frowned and stepped over to the trunk. Her brown hand reached out and touched the blue silk gown that rested on top. "This here dress belong to Miss Cecilia."

Abigail's face paled. "You mean the deaf child for whom the school was named?"

Virgie nodded. "Sweetest little thing I ever knew. And kind she was."

Helen frowned. "But I thought she died when she was a child."

Virgie shrugged and nodded. "Miss Cecilia pass away

when she was fifteen. But her mama let her go to the ball that year."

"Rather young," Abigail murmured.

The old lady nodded and sighed. "I reckon the old miss would have given that chile anything she wanted that year. They knew she was dying, you see."

"How sad." Tears pooled in Abigail's eyes.

Helen patted her arm. "Yes, very sad."

Abigail ran her hand over the silk. "I think I'd like to keep this one. I wouldn't like to cut it up." She lifted it from the trunk and laid it across a chair in the corner.

Virgie smiled at the next one. "This here belonged to Miss Claire. You should've seen her sashaying around like she the queen of Sheba, her golden curls bobbing up and down. She the only one of the children who didn't have black hair."

The tension in the room lifted as Virgie described Claire and Suzette, pointing out the dresses and where they wore each.

Helen breathed a sigh of relief. It would have been a shame to cancel the project of making the dresses over into costumes due to sentiment. Although Claire Quincy Bouvier had passed away years ago, Trent's Aunt Suzette still lived somewhere in France. An old lady now, Helen doubted she even remembered the gowns.

Patrick gave final instructions to his assistant, Stu Collins. He took a deep breath, relishing the scent of leather and oil, then glanced around the shop, making sure he hadn't forgotten anything. He tossed a wave at Stu and walked out the door. He made a quick stop at home to retrieve his already packed bag. An hour later he was on the train to Mimosa Junction.

It had been three weeks since he'd left his daughter

sobbing on the porch of Quincy School. He knew she'd be surprised to see him and as happy as he was that he could come back so soon.

He leaned back on the leather seat and glanced out the window at the countryside rolling by. He still wasn't sure what he was going to do about Molly. He wanted her home, but she was learning so much at the school. Would it really be fair to remove her from the program now? He sighed. Well, he had several months before he'd need to make a decision.

He dozed off and on, coming fully awake when the train pulled into Mimosa Junction. The sun was setting as he stepped onto the platform of the nearly empty station. He tipped his hat to a lady standing on the platform then headed for the livery.

A boy sat on a three-legged stool oiling a saddle. "'Evenin', Mr. Flannigan. Good to see you back."

Patrick smiled. "Good to be back. Are the horse and carriage I rented last time available?"

"Yes, sir." The boy jumped up, wiping his hands on his leather apron.

"No, I don't need them until morning. Just wanted to ask you to hold them for me. I'll need them for several days." After the arrangements were made, Patrick started toward the hotel. He walked down the dusty street. Most of the stores were closed already. Passing an empty building, he frowned. The sign said Mill's General Store. He was pretty sure it had been open for business three weeks ago. Pretty short time to shut down and empty out a store. A few doors down he noticed the hardware store was also empty. He continued on to the hotel and registered for a room. He left his luggage and came back downstairs, wondering if he should go back and get the rig and drive on out to the school. He glanced at his watch. No, definitely too late. He went into the dining room and ordered a meal.

When the waiter brought his food, Patrick said, "I noticed a couple of newly emptied buildings around town."

The waiter nodded. "Yes, sir, Mill's General Store and Tom's hardware shut down. They took their families and moved to Atlanta."

"Both of them?"

The waiter shrugged. "They were brothers. They decided to go in business together in the city."

"Rather sudden, wasn't it?"

"Oh. No, sir. They'd made their plans six months ago. A feller by the name of Watson bought the store. He's getting ready to remodel it before opening for business."

"What about the hardware store?"

The man shrugged. "No buyer as far as I know. Won't be the first time a building has stood deserted in this town."

Patrick thanked the man and turned his attention to the delicious meal, suddenly realizing he was hungry. He wished he'd left Atlanta earlier. He could have had dinner with Molly and Helen.

Now why had he included Helen in that thought? Come to think of it, he'd thought about her a lot lately. Well, why not? She was Molly's teacher and seemed to care a lot for his daughter. Of course he'd think about her.

But why did he smile or grin like an idiot when those thoughts of her came? Shoving the question to the back of his mind, he wondered if she'd have some time for him while he was here. She could tell him how Molly was doing and perhaps teach him some more signs. He wasn't doing too well on his own.

Maybe she'd like to go for a drive with him so they could have a nice long talk.

The last time he'd seen her, her soft blue eyes had seemed sad. Could she have been sorry to see him go?

He sighed. *Don't be ridiculous, Patrick Flannigan.* He continued to chide himself throughout dinner.

Chapter 6

Helen braided her long hair and wrapped the braids around her head, fastening them with hairpins. She'd decided with the work she'd be doing today, helping to move the girls into their rooms, the braids would work better than putting her hair in a bun.

She glanced in the mirror, turning her head this way and that. Besides, she rather liked the effect. If she had time to mess with braids every morning she might just stick with the hairstyle.

She gave a little laugh and shook her head at her silliness. What difference did it make anyway?

With a final glance to make sure her simple housedress was straight, she opened her door and nearly bumped into Charles Waverly, who stood with his hand raised to knock.

"Oops. I nearly knocked you in the head." He grinned and stepped back, letting her catch her breath.

Helen laughed. "You startled me. That's almost as bad."

"Sorry. P.J. wants you and me to put our heads together and come up with a more practical classroom schedule, now that we have more students and teachers coming soon.

Helen frowned. "We only have two new students so far, with three more coming in the next few months. By then, the school year will be ending and we'll have the whole summer to think about scheduling. Why is she in such a big hurry?"

Charles shook his head. "You know P.J. When she gets an idea in her head, she wants it done yesterday."

"True." Impatience surged through Helen, but she gave a chuckle as they walked to the stairs side by side and started down. "Well, we can't do anything about it this weekend. Let's each give it some thought and discuss it next weekend. Is that all right with you?"

"That's fine." He gave her a sideways glance and his eyes sparkled. "I like your new hairdo. It's very becoming."

Surprised, Helen felt heat surge over her cheeks. Charles wasn't one to hand out compliments. He generally tended to tease in the other direction. "Why, thank you. I wanted to make sure my hair stays out of the way while I'm working today."

They entered the dining room to find everyone seated. P.J. darted a pointed look in their direction. "Ah, here you are at last. If you'll take your seats, Howard was just about to say grace."

Helen hastened to her seat with Charles right behind her. He held her chair then hurried around to his place on the other side of the table.

Helen could hear P.J.'s shoe tapping. *My goodness, P.J. We're not in that big a hurry. Calm down.* She kept the thought to herself and bowed her head as Howard asked God's blessing on the food and on their day's endeavors.

They were halfway through the meal when Helen heard voices in the foyer. It sounded like…could it be? She finished her breakfast, trying not to cast darting glances toward the door.

She waited while the children filed out after their house parents. They were going to be moving their own things to the bedrooms once the furniture was in place. Some of the neighborhood women had been kind enough to make new quilts for the beds and bright scarves for their dressers. In the meantime, the two volunteers, Becky and Amy, would take them outside to play until time for the noon meal.

The sight that met her eyes as she stepped into the foyer made her heart leap. Patrick looked down at Molly, whose arms were wound tightly around his waist. The sparkle in Patrick's eyes matched the one in his daughter's as she gazed adoringly upward.

"I wasn't expecting you today, Papa." Her voice quivered.

"I wasn't sure I could make it, sweetheart, and I didn't want to raise your hopes then have to dash them." His glance drifted to Helen and the sparkle brightened even more, if that were possible.

"Good morning, Helen." His smile sent a thrill through Helen.

"Good morning to you, Patrick." She hoped he didn't misconstrue the lilt in her voice and think she had a personal interest in his presence. Because, of course, she didn't. She was simply happy for Molly's sake.

Molly tugged on his sleeve. "You're just in time to help move the furniture to my new room."

"Yes, I was just speaking to Albert about that very thing. In fact, I think I'll help with the others, too." He pulled one of her braids. "Is that all right with you, Miss Flannigan?"

Molly giggled. "All right. But we'll do something together later?"

"I promise we will." He stooped and kissed her on the cheek.

"I'll see you when it's time to eat, then." Her eyes were roving toward the door that had shut behind Amy.

"You can count on it." He grinned. "Now run along and join your friends, if you'd like."

After Molly ran outside, Patrick turned to Helen, grinning. "I'm assuming we won't be working together today?"

"Ummm. No." Helen laughed. "I'll be helping clean out the dormitories and then help the girls get settled in."

"Then, as Molly said, 'I'll see you when it's time to eat.' " He gave a slight bow and started up the stairs.

"The man is smitten."

Helen composed her expression before turning to face P.J. "Whatever do you mean?"

P.J. laughed. "Never mind. Did Charles speak to you about my request?"

"Yes, he did. We'll be thinking about it this coming week then get together next Saturday. Does that meet your approval?" Helen hoped the words didn't sound sarcastic, because she didn't intend them to be. At least, she didn't think so.

"Perfect! I have every confidence in the two of you to get this organized. Of course, you might want to get some input from Miss Wilson, as well, since she teaches two separate sign language classes."

"Yes, of course. You want the new schedule for next year?" Helen tried not to fidget, but she needed to get upstairs.

"Actually, I thought we'd go ahead and implement it as soon as the new teachers arrive." She looked down at her skirt and brushed at a nonexistent piece of lint.

Helen felt her mouth drop open and clamped it shut. She took a deep breath. "But that will be in late March. We'll be preparing for end of school testing and the program just weeks later."

P.J. patted Helen's arm. "I know, dear. But we really need to try out the new schedule, so if it doesn't work, we'll have the entire summer to fix it. Now I need to speak to Selma. I have every confidence in you and Charles." With a flutter of her fingers she charged toward the kitchen.

Helen sighed then shook her head and started up the stairs. P.J. could be trying at times, but she was an excellent director and most of her ideas worked perfectly. On the rare occasions they didn't, P.J. was the first to admit her mistake and start over again.

The morning passed swiftly, and although the work was tiring, Helen enjoyed visiting with Hannah Wilson, Felicity, and some of the neighbor ladies while she worked. She missed Abigail, who was usually right in the middle of any school work project, but she and Trent had gone to Atlanta on business.

Although they'd all taken periodic breaks, by the time Flora came upstairs banging on a cowbell to announce dinner was ready, the noon break was a welcome relief.

Laughter rang out through the dining room as they shared silly mishaps that occurred throughout the morning.

Helen had cringed when she'd heard the men teasing Patrick about his dandified looks in comparison with their work clothes. After all, Patrick hadn't known it was a work day, but she soon saw that he was a good sport and gave back as good as he got.

An hour later, refreshed and in good spirits, everyone was back at their tasks.

School had been held all week in the new third-floor

classrooms so that Albert and a few neighbors could transform the former classrooms into dorm rooms. By late afternoon, the touch-up work had been finished on Felicity's and Howard's living quarters and all the student rooms and were now ready for occupancy.

Molly and her roommate, Trudy, one of the new students, stood in their room and looked around with awe. Molly turned and gave Trudy a big hug. "Isn't it beautiful? And it's all ours, Trudy. We won't even have to worry about the little girls getting into our things."

Helen glanced at Patrick, who stood in the doorway, and they exchanged a smile.

Trudy gasped and stepped over to the washstand. Her hand reached out to touch the rose that adorned the porcelain washbowl. "Oh, Molly," she whispered. "We have our own pitcher and bowl, and they aren't even tin."

Helen choked back laughter. The tin pitchers and wash pans in the girls' dormitory had been what Felicity referred to as her bane of existence for years, and apparently the girls felt the same.

"All right, girls. As you can see, Sissy and Flora have filled the pitcher with warm water, so now would be a good time to clean up for supper. Sissy or Flora will empty them later and refill them in the morning. But you will be expected to clean up any splashed water. Can you manage that?"

"Yes, Miss Edwards." The girls echoed each other.

"Very well. You have twenty minutes before supper. We'll see you in the dining room."

She shut the door and waved at Patrick, who'd already headed for the stairs. She grinned as she went to freshen up. She'd bet he had no idea his red curls were dusted with plaster.

* * *

When Helen came downstairs, Patrick stood in the foyer talking to Howard and Charles. Molly stood beside him, her hand in his. He'd donned his suit coat and his hair was free of dust. It seemed as if Mr. Flannigan had done some freshening up, too.

All eyes turned in her direction. Patrick took a step toward her, but before he could speak, Charles offered his arm. "May I escort you in to supper, Helen?"

Disappointment clouded Patrick's eyes for a moment but disappeared so quickly that Helen wondered if she'd imagined it.

Not wanting to be rude, she took Charles's arm. "And who will escort Miss Molly in, I wonder?"

"Papa and I are going to the hotel for dinner, and…" Molly stopped at a touch from her father's hand.

"Oh, I see." She'd hoped for an opportunity to speak with Patrick after supper and ask how his signing was coming along. "In that case, I'll see you when you get back, Molly."

She turned away before they could see the disappointment that surely showed in her eyes.

Patrick tried to keep his attitude cheerful for Molly's sake, but the memory of Helen holding Charles Waverly's arm didn't make it easy.

Was Waverly simply being a gentleman or was he interested in Helen romantically? He couldn't blame the man if he was. After all, she was a beautiful woman as well as a kind and gracious lady. The real question was whether Helen returned the man's interest. If interest it was.

"Papa, you're not listening to me." Molly frowned and looked about to cry.

Contrite, Patrick pulled up in front of the hotel. "I'm sorry, angel. I guess my mind did wander a little."

He walked around and helped her down then proffered his arm.

A shy smile tipped her lips. "I like it when you treat me like I'm all grown up."

"Well, I'm practicing for when you become a grown-up young lady." He patted her hand. "But let's hold that off for a few years."

She giggled then pressed her lips together as they walked into the lobby and crossed to the dining room.

The waiter remembered Molly from the last time and delighted her by addressing her as Miss Flannigan.

Halfway through her chocolate cake, she yawned and sighed. "I'm sorry, Papa."

"Think nothing of it, sweetheart. We've had a busy day." He stretched his mouth open, covering it with his hand. "There, you see? I'm sleepy, too."

She laughed. "Oh, Papa. You just pretended to yawn."

"You caught me." He grinned. "What do you say? Let's head back to the school so you can try out that new bedroom. I'll bet Trudy's lonely there all alone."

"Oh. You may be right." She folded her napkin and laid it on the table then stood.

Before they were out of town, her head sank onto Patrick's shoulder.

She roused enough to walk inside when they arrived at the school.

Helen met them at the door. "Ah, a sleepy girl, I see."

Molly yawned. "I slept all the way from the hotel, Miss Edwards."

Patrick returned Molly's hug. "See you in the morning. I'll drive you and Trudy to church, if you like."

"Oh, yes. I'd better go tell her." She started to the stairs then turned. "Good night, Papa. Good night, Miss Edwards."

He glanced at Helen, surprised to see distress on her face.

"Is something wrong?" he asked.

"Patrick, you can't take someone else's child on a drive unless their parents have left written permission for you to do so." She bit her lip.

"Oh, it never occurred to me." What an idiot he was. "It should have. I know I wouldn't want Molly to leave the school with someone I hadn't met."

She nodded.

"I hate to disappoint the girls after I've promised." He glanced at her. "Do you think it would be all right, if a member of the staff went along?"

"I think so. You'd need to ask Miss Wellington." P.J. could be pretty strict where the children were concerned.

"Actually, I was going to ask you if you would ride with us anyway. That is, unless you've agreed to go with someone else." Like Waverly.

"Yes, I could go. I usually ride in the wagon with the children, but they have plenty of other adults riding with them." She lowered her lashes. "I wouldn't want to disappoint Molly and Trudy. That is, of course, if P.J. gives her approval."

Moonlight streamed through the door and touched her hair with gold. Patrick wanted to caress the silky braids that wound around her head.

"Like I said, I was going to ask you before. So please come with us even if Miss Wellington won't allow Trudy to go."

A blush tinged her cheeks and she smiled. "Then I'll see you in the morning, and I hope Trudy will be with us on the drive. Good night, Patrick."

He stood there for a moment after she'd closed the door. Happiness surged through him. And this time, it wasn't mixed with guilt. Somehow he knew Maureen wouldn't mind.

Chapter 7

The silence in the parlor had gone on too long. Helen opened her mouth to ask Charles to please repeat his last statement, but the sudden chiming of the clock gave her another precious moment of respite.

Charles sat across from her, the scheduling book on his lap. His face was flushed and seemed to grow redder by the moment.

Oh dear, she hadn't heard him wrong. He'd said his affection for her had transcended friendship sometime ago and could she possibly accept him as a suitor.

She swallowed past a sudden lump in her throat. How could she let him down without crushing his ego? She cleared her throat. "I'm not quite sure what to say, Charles. This is totally unexpected. Could you give me some time to think about it?

Relief tinged with hope ran across his face and he

smiled. "Of course. I realize it's rather sudden. After all, we've been friends and colleagues for years."

"Yes, yes, that's right." *Coward. Just tell him you don't think of him in any other way. Don't prolong his anxiety.*

"How long do you think you'll need to consider the idea?"

She dabbed the sudden moisture from her chin and forehead, hoping he didn't notice. "Well, I'm not sure. I'll let you know."

Charles frowned. Oh dear. His reaction was so unlike the happy-go-lucky jokester she knew who could make her laugh even when she didn't feel like it. She brightened. Maybe this was another of his jokes. She threw him a hopeful look; but no, he was serious. It was written all over his face.

She stood. "I believe we have the schedule all ready for P.J., don't you agree?"

He glanced at the schedule and nodded. His countenance was a picture of disappointment. "Yes, I think so." He rose. "I hope I haven't caused you distress, Helen."

"Oh no. No, I'm honored. Who wouldn't be? And you know I'm fond of you. But I need to think about it." She threw a rather weak smile in his general direction. "Now we'd better take this to P.J. and let her look it over."

"Yes, of course." He crossed to the door and held it open while she passed through.

After leaving the schedule with P.J., Helen murmured a quick good-bye to the director and Charles and scurried up to her room, almost dizzy from the encounter with Charles. At least he'd waited until the schedule was finished before blurting out the unwelcome revelation.

Helen eased into the rocking chair by her window and leaned back. She'd hoped Patrick might visit again this weekend, but now she was glad he hadn't. What if he'd noticed the glances Charles had begun to cast in her direction? She shut her eyes tightly. And what if he had? Patrick had never indicated by word or expression that he thought of her as anything but Molly's teacher.

She, on the other hand, couldn't deny her growing attraction to Patrick Flannigan. She sighed. Well, she could just get over it. There wouldn't have been any hope for the two of them even if he was interested in her. He lived and worked in Atlanta and her life work, the passion of her life, was right here at Quincy School. It was impossible.

Perhaps she should consider Charles's request. They had the same goals and interests in life. And she did care for him. He'd been a dear friend for years. It wasn't everyone who could make her laugh. And anyone could see he was quite handsome. So what if the sight of him didn't send her heart into double beats and turn her knees to jelly. Those feelings would likely come if they were married. She groaned. She wouldn't think about that now. She had more important things to consider. Like the new student who would arrive next week. She'd arrive just in time to try out for a part in the Easter cantata.

The cantata itself wouldn't require much thought on her part. Abigail would be in charge of that. She'd done such a wonderful job on the Christmas concert and play that her election as drama and concert director had been unanimous. And after the Christmas play, the magical moment came when Abigail and Trent had exchanged their wedding vows.

Moisture pooled in Helen's eyes. Would she ever experience the joy that had radiated from both bride and groom on that day? Their faces had glowed with it. She closed her eyes again and tried to picture herself walking down the aisle toward a beaming Charles, but the fantasy groom that stood there waiting for her had taken on the form and countenance of Patrick Flannigan.

Her eyes flew open. This was ridiculous. She might as well find something constructive to do if her rest was going to bombard her with romantic fantasies that would never come to pass. So much for the relaxing weekend she'd hoped for.

She went to her writing table and picked up a small stack of papers that still needed to be graded. She'd planned to do it here, but perhaps her classroom would help her keep her mind on sensible things.

She climbed the stairs to the third floor where the smell of new wood and fresh paint still permeated the air. She stepped inside her classroom and stood in the doorway, beholding with satisfaction the smooth oak cupboards that housed supplies and books. She wondered what old Mrs. Quincy would think of her school today. Six new desks had been added in anticipation of the new students that were expected and perhaps others who hadn't enrolled yet.

Next year would be different, all right. One of the students was a thirteen-year-old boy named Roger Brumley, who'd had no formal schooling. He had partial sight and very little hearing. She only hoped they could help him. The mother of a nine-year-old deaf-blind boy had applied only to change her mind and withdraw the application. Helen hoped she'd found another school and hadn't decided to keep him at home.

With a sigh, Helen sat at her desk and began to grade the history papers. As she took one from the stack, she noticed a stiff piece of braille paper. Lily Ann. Apparently she'd decided it was time to get back to work learning to write. Helen ran her hand over the dots the child had made with her stylus. She wanted to help Lily, but unfortunately the girl was further along in her braille studies than Helen.

"All right, Lily Ann," she whispered in the empty room. "I'll get the book out and do my best."

She finished grading the papers and stacked them neatly on her desk with a paperweight on top. She stood and picked up Lily Ann's paper and went to one of the cupboards. She took the braille instruction book out and headed for the door.

After lunch, she returned to her room and sat by the window. She had several hours to study the braille book. Helen hoped she'd learn some new words in that time.

She suddenly realized she hadn't thought of Patrick or Charles for hours.

A sigh escaped her lips. Unfortunately, the problem hadn't gone away. She had to decide what to do about Charles. And in all fairness to him, she shouldn't prolong the decision.

Patrick gave the piece of luggage another swipe with a soft cloth and looked the enormous black bag over with a critical eye.

Philip Taney had ordered the bag specially made to hold all his belongings as he traveled through Europe on his year abroad.

"You see," the young man had explained, "I don't want to have to worry about handling two or three bags everywhere I go."

"But this one might get heavy, don't you think?" Patrick had eyed the lad with some amusement.

Philip had shrugged. "I'm strong. Besides, my valet will be with me."

Patrick chuckled now, thinking of the boy who'd spent a fairly large amount of money to get the bag exactly as he wanted it. It wouldn't surprise Patrick a bit if Taney ended up selling or discarding the magnificent piece for something more practical, valet or not. But that wasn't his business. The spoiled young man was used to getting what he thought he wanted, and his wealthy father didn't seem to mind footing the bill.

He placed the bag on a shelf behind the counter and glanced at his watch. He'd hoped to be finished early today so he could catch the early train to Mimosa Junction. He hadn't seen Molly in two weeks. He grinned as a pair of light blue eyes flashed into his mind instead of his daughter's dark blue ones.

He'd been careful not to make his attraction to Helen known to her just yet. For one thing, if she didn't return his interest, it could be awkward since she was Molly's teacher. However, he was afraid he might have been a little too distant the last few times he was there. Much to his chagrin, he'd noticed on his last visit that Charles Waverly acted a little too chummy with Helen. Of course, he'd also noticed she'd seemed uncomfortable with the man's attention. Perhaps it was time to try a little subtle attention of his own.

He was about to close up shop when Philip Taney charged in with a friend in tow.

"Hello, Patrick. This is my friend and soon-to-be fellow traveler, Ronald Simmons. Can you show him my bag?"

Patrick turned and took the bag off the shelf. "Here you go. All finished."

Philip took the bag and held it out for his friend's inspection. "See? What did I tell you?"

"That's perfect." The tall young man looked over at Patrick. "Can you make one just like it for me?"

"I'd be happy to. I'll start on it next week."

The boy's face fell. "But we're leaving Tuesday."

Patrick sighed. It wouldn't do to pass up business when his shop was just starting to flourish. But if he agreed, it would mean he'd have to skip his planned visit to the school.

"All right. If you can pay me ahead of time, I'll get started on it tomorrow."

The deal made, Taney took his bag and the two left Patrick standing there filled with dismay.

Perhaps he should have refused. The lad could have purchased another bag either at his store or elsewhere. But then, what sort of reputation would his shop have? He shook his head. No, he'd done the right thing. He needed to make sure his finances were secure for Molly's sake.

The next week crawled by, but at last he found himself getting off the train at Mimosa Junction. He noticed activity around the general store and a brand-new sign hanging above the door that said Watson's Mercantile. So the new owner was getting the store ready for business.

He wondered if the hardware store had a buyer yet. It would be just the right size for his leather shop. A thrill shot threw him at the thought. Now why would he think of something like that? He chuckled—a very nervous sounding chuckle. He had a thriving business in Atlanta. He wasn't looking for a change. Of course, if he was, Mimosa Junction wouldn't be a bad choice. The junction was just what its name implied, and customers came from miles away in three different directions. He gave another short laugh. But he wasn't considering a change in location, was he?

The next morning he arrived at the Cecilia Quincy School for the Deaf just in time to have breakfast with his daughter.

"Papa, what are we going to do today? Can we go for a drive in the carriage?" Molly's exuberance rang across the table.

"I should hope so. It's a beautiful spring day." March had indeed come in like a lamb, as the saying went.

"Trudy's parents signed a permission note so she can go with us." She darted a look at her friend and roommate.

Trudy blushed, but hope filled her warm brown eyes.

"If it's all right with the director, I think that's a mighty fine idea." Patrick winked at Molly then at Trudy. Both girls giggled.

After breakfast, Patrick waited in the foyer while the girls helped clear the table. Helen walked out, with Charles Waverly following closely behind.

"Miss Edwards?" Although they'd been on a first name basis for a while, he was reluctant to use her first name around the other teachers.

She smiled and stopped beside him. "Yes, Mr. Flannigan?"

Charles stood there as if unsure what to do. Patrick gave him a polite nod then turned to address Helen.

"I wondered if you'd agree to accompany the girls and me on our drive." Helen blushed and he hastened to say, "I mean, as a chaperone of sorts."

Charles stiffened. "Weren't we going to go over the schedule again, Helen?"

"P.J. seemed quite satisfied with the last version." Helen gave him a gentle smile. "I don't think it's necessary to change anything, do you?"

"I guess not." He glanced from Helen to Patrick. "Well then, I'll see you at noon."

Patrick watched the man walk away, wondering whether to feel pity or irritation.

"I'd be more than happy to go along as a chaperone." She cast a worried glance after Charles.

"I'm sorry if I caused a problem for you." Perhaps

there was more between those two than he'd realized. The thought sent disappointment twisting through him.

Helen gave a sad smile. "No, the problem was already there, and I'm afraid it's my own fault for not taking care of it before now."

"I see." He didn't see at all but was relieved that she considered Waverly a problem that needed to be taken care of. "Here come the girls now."

"Papa! We're ready to go." Molly grabbed Helen's hand. "Will you come with us, Miss Edwards?"

Helen laughed. "Your father just asked me the same thing, and I said yes."

Both girls squealed with delight and grabbed her hands. The three of them went outside and down the stairs, their hands swinging between them as Patrick followed behind, feeling rather left out.

Patrick grinned when Molly and Trudy climbed into the backseat. Just what he had hoped they'd do.

The sun was shining brightly by the time they drove away. Patrick took every side road he came across in order to lengthen their drive.

"Papa, are you lost?" Molly's worried voice from the back seat brought him to his senses.

"No, sweetheart. Not at all." He turned and gave her a reassuring smile, knowing his assurances were true. "I'm heading back to the main road now."

"Well, I'm getting hungry. It must be almost dinner time," Molly said. "Are you hungry, Trudy?"

"Well, yes." Trudy blushed.

"I'm hungry, too, girls." He grinned over his shoulder. "How about we go get something to eat at the hotel?"

"Fried chicken, Papa?" Molly asked.

"You mean the fried chicken that's almost as good as Cook's?"

Molly glanced at Trudy. "It's almost as good, but we mustn't tell Cook that, all right?"

"Okay. She'd probably never cook fried chicken for us again."

A choking sound came from Helen's direction. "Now, girls, you make Cook sound vain and she isn't at all."

"Yes, ma'am." Molly nodded. "But she is a little bit vain about her fried chicken."

Helen threw her head back slightly and laughed again. Patrick's breath caught. Was anyone ever so lovely?

Chapter 8

Helen tapped on the director's door. When asked to come in, she opened the door and stepped into the office. The other teachers and both house parents were already seated, as was a tall and regal appearing young girl who sat with chin up and ankles crossed.

Helen glanced at P.J., who gave her a tight smile and nodded to the chair next to the new student. "Miss Edwards, this is Margaret Long. Margaret, Miss Edwards is our English, history, and geography teacher."

Helen smiled and offered her hand, which the girl gripped and released as though it might bite.

Helen sat and turned to the girl, enunciating clearly. "I'm very pleased to welcome you to our school, Margaret. Do you go by Meg or Peggy?"

The girl lifted her chin more and peered down her nose at Helen. "Certainly not. You may call me Margaret." The girl's speech lacked the singsong tone often noticed in the speech of the deaf. But goodness, how did the child learn to be so haughty in only twelve years?

Helen leaned back and lifted her brow at Hannah, who ducked her head to hide a smile.

Goodness. The girl was only twelve?

P.J. cleared her throat. "It seems that Margaret is much more advanced than our other students, Miss Edwards. There may need to be some one-on-one teaching."

Margaret, who apparently had been following the conversation quite well, raised her hand.

"Yes, Margaret?" P.J.'s eyes weren't exactly narrowed, but Helen had seen that expression before. She could only wonder what had transpired before she arrived in the room.

"If your teachers aren't qualified to teach me, I'm quite capable of learning from books on my own."

Helen felt her mouth drop open and quickly pressed her lips together. The little rascal.

P.J. took a deep breath and let it out slowly. "Miss Long, the teachers at Quincy School are quite capable of teaching you anything you need to learn."

Margaret sniffed audibly and tossed her head. "Yes, ma'am. If you say so."

"I do." P.J. glanced at Felicity. "Will you please get Margaret settled in and ask one of the other girls to show her around? She can meet the rest of the children at supper."

Felicity stood. "Of course. Come with me, dear. You'll feel right at home before long."

Margaret stood and sent the housemother a benevolent glance but remained silent and followed her out of the room.

The moment the door shut behind them, Charles turned

to P.J. "Are you sure she's only twelve? How did she learn to be such a snob in twelve years?"

P.J. sighed. "She had a good teacher. You didn't meet the mother. You will next weekend. Then you can judge for yourself."

Howard shook his head. "I hope she doesn't have a brother headed our way."

Charles laughed and the two men walked out together.

"What do you think, Helen?" P.J. threw her a curious look.

"Well, it's a little too soon for me to tell." Helen bit her lip. "Perhaps her attitude is a covering for something that bothers her."

P.J. nodded. "Good. You're going for mercy instead of judgment. Somehow I knew I could count on you to do that." She turned to Hannah. "Take a lesson from Helen, my dear. She's a wonderful role model for any teacher."

Hannah who only recently finished her training and was teaching for the first time, smiled shyly. "Yes, I know."

"Oh, you two. You're going to make me cry or else make me conceited." Helen laughed. "I'd better get upstairs and see how the other girls react to our newest addition."

She arrived at the top of the stairs to see Felicity leave one of the nicer bedrooms and shut the door behind her.

Felicity stopped when she saw Helen and whispered, "Her parents insisted that she have a private room. P.J. told her it would depend on how many students enroll. But for now, at least, Miss Long is ensconced in her private palace and holding suit."

"What do you mean?" Helen felt queasy.

Felicity motioned toward the door. "See for yourself." She walked away.

Helen tapped on the door and opened it.

Margaret sat in the overstuffed chair in the corner, while

Trudy and Molly unpacked her trunk. She glanced at Helen then turned back to the girls.

"Be careful. That's my favorite dress. It needs to be hung on a hanger and smoothed down."

"What's going on here?" Helen stepped into the room and took the green velvet dress from Trudy.

"We're helping Margaret, Miss Edwards," Molly said. "She gets headaches when she travels."

"In that case, it might be best if you two return to your own room and let Margaret lie down and rest. She can unpack her trunk later."

The girls scurried out and Helen laid the dress back in the trunk. She couldn't help but notice all the dresses. "If you need help, Margaret, I'll send one of the maids up to help you when they're not busy. But you need to realize that we expect the students to take care of their own personal needs as much as possible."

The girl's eyes shot daggers at Helen and when she spoke her voice was scornful. "In my old school, I had my own personal maid."

"That may very well be, my dear." Helen kept her face pleasant. "But that's not the way we operate here."

"Fine, you may leave now. I want to rest." Margaret clamped her lips together and turned her back, but not before Helen noticed the tears that had filled her eyes.

Helen shook her head and left the room, shutting the door softly. She knew Margaret's parents had moved to Georgia from Alabama and hadn't wanted their daughter to be so far away from them. Was the girl simply spoiled or was she perhaps brokenhearted over leaving dear friends and beloved teachers?

Helen sighed. Time would tell. In the meantime, she had no intention of allowing Molly and Trudy to become the girl's slaves, willing or unwilling.

* * *

"Pat! Pat Flannigan!"

Patrick swung around and his heart leapt. Jane Fuller, a friend of Maureen's, waved from across the street. Her red hair hung in curls below a fashionable sapphire-blue hat.

He waited while she made her way across the busy street, closing his eyes when a boy on a bicycle dodged to miss her.

Laughing, she stepped upon the sidewalk and grabbed his arm. "Pat, it's so wonderful to see you."

"Jane, I thought that bike had you for sure. I see you're still taking crazy risks."

She giggled and dropped his arm. "Why haven't you been to see me, you naughty boy? It's been over a year."

Had it really been that long? He sighed. How could he tell her that the sight of her caused him to miss Maureen that much more?

"It's all right. I understand." She touched his arm. "But Pat, it's been more than two years. Maureen wouldn't want you to keep grieving."

"I know. And I'm not, really." He smiled. "I guess I'll always miss her. She was my childhood sweetheart, you know. Sometimes, I think that's what I remember the most."

"But she'd want you to get on with your life. Fall in love again. Get married." She paused and looked at him. "Uh oh. What's the red face about? There is someone?"

"Well, maybe. I'm not sure." He frowned and stumbled for words.

Jane tilted her head until she could look into his eyes. "Hmmm. This sounds very interesting. Too interesting to talk about in the middle of the sidewalk. Come to dinner tonight? Michael would love to see you."

"I'm sorry. I have an order that needs to be filled before

tomorrow. I'll be working late." He hesitated then went on. "But I'm on my way to the café around the corner. Come eat lunch with me."

She tilted her head for a moment. "I think I will." She turned and motioned to her carriage driver to follow then took Patrick's arm.

A few minutes later, they were settled at a neat table, covered with a red and white tablecloth.

He tapped the table. "Not the fanciest place in town, but it's clean and the food is good."

"Never mind the food. I want to hear about the woman you're in love with." She leaned forward and looked intently across the table at him.

Patrick laughed. "Let's order first. I'm starving."

"Oh, all right." She flashed a smile at the waiter and ordered chicken salad and lemonade.

"Now, tell me." She folded her hands on the table.

Patrick shook his head. "There's not a lot to tell. I've fallen for one of the teachers at Molly's school."

"Really?" Surprise filled her eyes. "Well, does she feel the same about you?"

Their food arrived. After the waiter left, Jane bowed her head and Patrick prayed over the meal.

She took a bite of her salad then glanced up. "Well?"

"I've no idea." He took a bite of his roast beef.

"Oh, Pat. Don't tell me you haven't spoken to her about it."

"All right, I won't tell you." He grinned.

Laughter pealed from her throat. "I've never known you to be shy."

"It's not shyness." He laid his fork on the plate and leaned back, suddenly without appetite.

"At first, you see, I felt guilty. Like I was betraying

Maureen. But lately, I realize that, like you said, Maureen would want me to marry again."

"Then what's the problem?" Her eyes widened. "Do you doubt she'd be a good mother to Molly?"

"No, Molly adores her and she seems to feel the same way." He heaved a sigh. "I'm just not sure it would work. My business is here and she's dedicated to the children at the school."

"Oh, is that all?" She sipped her lemonade then grinned. "Ask her. If she cares about you, she'll leave that school in the blink of an eye."

"But would it be right for me to ask her to do that? It's obvious she loves her work."

"Well, she'll still have her work. She can teach Molly." Jane took another sip. "There you are. The perfect solution. Now you can tell her how you feel about her."

Later, as Patrick worked at his bench, his thoughts turned back to their conversation. He wasn't sure whether to be amused at Jane's simple assessment of the situation or be irritated at her lack of understanding. It didn't really matter, he supposed. The situation was still the same.

After thinking over Margaret's educational needs, P.J. determined that although she was so far ahead, she would continue with the other students in Helen's classroom for the rest of the year, with some additional reading and essays to keep her from becoming bored. She could work at her own level in Charles's mathematic and science classes. Over the summer, Helen and Hannah would work out Margaret's classroom schedule for the following year.

The week following Margaret's arrival went well. She was respectful to the teachers and made friends with all the other children.

Helen left her classroom on Friday with a breath of relief. They'd all misjudged the child. She'd probably been tired from traveling and that had caused her temporary behavior problem.

Over the weekend, she noticed Margaret, Molly, and Trudy with their heads together several times. They seemed to be establishing their own little circle of friends but were still friendly with the other children.

Helen went looking for Margaret after church on Sunday. She found her and the other girls talking beneath one of the magnolia trees in front of the house. Helen breathed in the lemony, sweet scent of the fresh blooms in appreciation. She loved the scent of magnolia.

The girls glanced up as she approached and for an instant Helen saw the look of animosity in Margaret's eyes; just as quickly, it was gone. Perhaps she'd imagined it.

"Were you looking for us, Miss Edwards?" Margaret flashed a sweet smile.

"As a matter of fact, I was looking for *you*, Margaret." She sank down on the soft green grass beside them and tucked her skirt underneath her leg. "Did Trudy and Molly mention the Easter cantata?"

"Why yes, they did." A flicker of something flashed in her eyes, but once again it was gone. "I think it's wonderful that Lily Ann is singing the lead part."

"Yes, our Lily has a beautiful voice. But so do the rest of the students." She smiled at Molly and Trudy then turned to Margaret. "Would you like to sing in the choir, dear?"

"Oh, could I?" Her voice lilted with excitement. "I'd really like that."

"Wonderful, we're having practice tomorrow afternoon at two." Helen rose from the soft ground and inhaled the fragrant air once more. "You girls need to get washed up for dinner. It won't be long now."

"Yes, Miss Edwards," they chorused. She smiled and

went back inside. How nice to see them getting along so well. Margaret was nearly a year older than the other two girls, but they were close enough in age to enjoy each other's company.

Lily Ann was sitting on a bench in the parlor, alone. Her home was nearby and she usually went home on the weekends, but this Sunday her parents were away. She glanced up. "Hello, Miss Edwards."

"Lily Ann, why are you sitting here by yourself? Don't you feel well?" Helen reached over and felt the child's forehead. "You don't seem to have a fever."

"I'm not sick. I'm just sitting here." She tapped her fingers on the bench.

"Would you like for me to read you a story, dear?" Lily Ann loved books and her braille skills weren't up to the level of the books she wanted to read.

She drew in a breath. "Oh yes, ma'am."

"All right. I think we'll have time for a story after dinner." She gave Lily a hug. "Your voice all fine-tuned for tomorrow's cantata practice?"

"I don't know." Lily whispered the words and her sightless eyes blinked fast.

"Lily, are you crying?" Helen peered closely, but no tears were visible.

"No, I'm not crying." Once again, her eyes began to blink. It seemed more a nervous reaction than tears.

"Are you sure something's not wrong, Lily?"

"Yes ma'am, I'm sure." She stood. "May I be excused? Sissy said I could help set the table."

"Yes, of course. And don't forget. We have a story-reading appointment right after dinner."

She watched the girl walk away toward the kitchen. She was such a little slip of a child. And usually cheerful. It wasn't like her to appear melancholy. Helen scoffed at herself. Lily Ann most likely just missed her parents. And Helen needed to stop looking for trouble where there was none.

"Helen." At the sound of her name, Helen groaned as Charles walked across the foyer from the library. At least this was one problem she hadn't imagined.

"Charles, could we speak privately later? Perhaps after supper?"

"Yes, of course. Shall we take a stroll down the lane?" His eyes held both hope and dread.

After their walk, his eyes would only hold one emotion. It was time she stopped delaying the inevitable.

Dread filled Helen's heart all during supper. She only hoped Charles wouldn't be too hurt at what she had to say. When the meal was over, she and Charles walked down the lane together. When they stopped beneath one of the live oaks, she looked up into his eyes.

Charles sighed. "Your answer is no?"

"I wish it could be yes, but I don't feel that way about you, Charles. I consider you a dear friend and I hope we can remain so."

He smiled and, leaning forward, planted a kiss on top of her head. "We'll always be friends, Helen. I regret putting you in this position. Let's not mention it again."

At bedtime, as she sank into her soft mattress, she thanked the Lord for giving her the courage to at least set this one matter straight.

Chapter 9

Excitement rippled across the new auditorium and the children filed backstage, getting ready for the practice.

Helen stood in the doorway and glanced over the huge room, envisioning chairs lined up side by side in rows from back to front. She gave a little chuckle. More than likely there would be about ten rows for the school staff, including the teachers, the students, and their families.

Helen headed for the dozen or so chairs that had been brought in for those who wanted to watch the practice. She sat beside Abigail, who was glancing over a list of students who'd volunteered to be in the cantata. Worry was written all over her face.

"Is anything wrong?" Helen hoped not. They only had a short time to get the musical together.

Abigail looked up. She shook her head. "I'm not sure. Lily Ann withdrew from the cantata."

"What? But why?" The little girl loved to sing and had been looking forward to her solo as well as the acting itself.

"She said she didn't want to do it." Abigail tapped her pencil against the chair beside her. "Did she seem melancholy while I was away?"

Abigail and Lily Ann had grown very close during the time Abigail had taught the child. She'd been happy when Trent and Abigail married, but she missed her teacher very much.

"No, she seemed fine." Helen hesitated. "But, come to think of it, she was behaving a little strangely yesterday. Especially when I asked her about practice."

"I see…. Well, no, I don't see." Abigail heaved a sigh. "I'm going to ask Beth to sing Lily Ann's part today, but I don't want to replace her just yet."

"I think that's a good idea." Helen nodded. Elizabeth Thompson, one of the older girls, had partial hearing and seemed to stay with the melody quite well. "And Beth won't be that disappointed if Lily Ann changes her mind."

Abigail smiled and glanced at the girl going up the side steps to the stage. "No, our Beth hasn't a competitive bone in her body."

"Have you met the new girl, yet?"

"Margaret? Yes, she's going to sing before we begin the practice. I need to know where to place her."

At Abigail's signal, Felicity sat at the piano. She nodded toward the wings, and Margaret walked onto the stage.

Silence fell across the listeners as Margaret sang "Silent Night."

Helen listened in awe. The girl's voice was beautiful. She glanced at Abigail, who seemed as mesmerized as Helen.

Margaret sang the last note and stood waiting.

"Thank you, Margaret. I'm putting you in the soprano section for now."

The girl smiled and walked off the stage.

Abigail turned to Helen. "Well, if Lily Ann doesn't sing the lead, at least I know who'll take her place."

Helen caught her breath, feeling like she'd been punched in the stomach. "Oh no." Could Margaret have had something to do with Lily Ann withdrawing? Surely not. Helen closed her eyes. She was imagining things about the new girl again.

Abigail cast a sharp look in her direction. "What? Oh no, what?"

Should she say something? But what if she was being overly suspicious and Margaret was innocent?

"Nothing. I just had a thought." She turned as Beth took her place on stage while the others lined up behind her. Today they were practicing the songs only.

Helen couldn't keep her glance from drifting to Margaret, who stood with the other sopranos, a look of total sweetness on her face.

Finally, Abigail stood. "Very good. We'll need to practice at least three times a week. So let's plan on Mondays, Wednesdays, and Fridays at four."

"Yes, Miz Quincy." The voices chorused from off the stage.

"But remember, if you should fall behind in your schoolwork, you will be out of the cantata."

They filed off the stage—some to do homework they'd put off, others to play outside until supper.

Uneasiness bit at Helen as she said good-bye to Abigail and went to the parlor in search of Virgie.

Virgie sat in her favorite wing chair, brushing Lily Ann's hair. They both glanced up as Helen entered and sat in a rocker across from them.

"We missed you at practice, Lily Ann."

Lily Ann darted a glance at Virgie, who pressed her lips together and began braiding Lily Ann's silky brown hair. "You goin' to answer Miz Helen?"

Lily Ann hiccuped. "Excuse me." She looked up beneath long lashes. "I'm not going to be in the Easter cantata."

Helen nodded. "Yes, Miss Abigail told me. Is anything wrong?"

Panic seized her face, but she shook her head. "No, ma'am."

Helen glanced at Virgie, who gave a shake of her head. Helen nodded. They'd talk later.

After supper, Helen made a beeline for the parlor where she found Virgie waiting for her.

"All right. What's going on?"

Virgie sighed. "I wish I knew. Something's got that little gal spooked."

"But she wouldn't tell you anything?"

"Not with words, she didn't." Pain crossed Virgie's thin brown face. "But something's bothering our Lily girl. So what are we going to do about it?"

Darkness enshrouded Helen's thoughts as anger rose like a thundercloud in her heart. Why would anyone wish to cause that precious child pain?

Helen jumped up. "I'm not sure what's going on, but I have a pretty good idea who might be behind it." Her fingers balled into fists.

Virgie stood and stepped over to her, worry filling her faded brown eyes. "Miz Helen, honey, don't let sin get aholt of you, now. Lift Lily Ann and whatever's in your mind up to the Lord. He love that little angel more than we do." She placed both hands on Helen's shoulders and gave her a gentle shake. "And if someone's causing her grief, well, the Lord love them, too. And He knows how to make it all come out right."

Helen bit her lip and nodded. "Thank you, Virgie. I'm sure you're right. I think I need to go upstairs and try to calm down.

Calm, however, was the last thing Helen felt as she paced her room. She was almost certain Molly and Trudy knew what was going on, and she was tempted to charge into their room and demand they tell her. But something held her back, and she was pretty sure it was God. She knew in her heart Virgie was right, but so far Helen had been unable to calm the turmoil inside her.

She dropped into the rocking chair and put her face in her hands. "Lord, forgive me for this uncontrolled anger. Please calm me down and show me what You want me to do."

At first, she sensed no change, but gradually, as she stayed in God's presence, peace like a warm cloak fell upon her. She breathed in a deep, welcome breath of surrender and let it flow back out through her lips.

While her class studied their history chapter, Helen looked over papers the children had turned in at the beginning of class.

Thursdays were usually the worst day of the week, with the students tired and ready for their weekend to begin. But they'd been model students all day, without even one scuffle or argument.

She glanced up from her desk and scanned the room in case anyone needed help. Every head was bent over in study except for Trudy's and Molly's.

Helen stood and walked over to Trudy's desk. Her book was closed and she stared straight ahead. Helen touched her on the shoulder and Trudy glanced up. Fear clouded her eyes.

"Why aren't you working, Trudy?" Instead of speaking, the girl signed, "I don't want to."

What? She didn't want to? Perhaps Helen misunderstood.

"Are you having trouble with the reading?" She frowned as she questioned Trudy.

Trudy shook her head and darted a glance at Molly, who sat at the next desk.

With dread in her heart, Helen stepped over to Molly's desk and sighed. Molly's book was also closed.

Helen touched her hand to get her attention. When Molly looked up, her eyes pooled with tears.

Helen tried to keep her face composed. "You don't wish to study, either?"

Molly shook her head.

"You realize we have an important test tomorrow?" Helen tapped her foot on the floor.

Molly nodded.

Helplessness washed over Helen. How could she handle something she didn't understand?

She walked over to Margaret's desk expecting a repeat of the disobedience. Margaret's book was open and she perused the page intently. She glanced up and smiled. Anyone would think she was totally innocent. Helen didn't believe that for a moment. Somehow she was controlling the other girls. But how?

Instructing Molly and Trudy to remain at their desks at the end of class, she returned to the papers she'd been grading.

She'd dealt with defiance before, but this was something different. *Lord, show me what to do and guide me as I speak to these girls.*

When the class filed out the door, Helen's glance happened to fall on Margaret just as she looked back at Molly and Trudy and her eyes sent a silent message. Helen clamped her lips together.

She motioned to the two girls to come up front and stand in front of her desk.

"All right, girls. This behavior isn't like you at all. I know something is wrong, and I don't believe it's your fault. Is someone bullying you in any way?"

Alarm sprung into both girls' eyes, and they both shook their heads vehemently.

"You can tell me. I won't let anyone harm you." She glanced from Molly to Trudy. "I promise. Please tell me what's going on."

Both girls stood silently, their faces pictures of misery.

Helen sighed. "Very well. I have no choice but to keep you in detention for an hour every day until you explain your conduct."

"But, Miss Edwards"—Molly clamped her hands over her mouth and signed—"what about our homework?"

"What about it? You'll work on it during detention. If you can't complete it in that time you will still have an hour before supper."

"But, but"—Trudy caught herself and signed— "the cantata?"

"I suppose you'll both have to drop out since you can't get to practice." At the pain on their faces, Helen wanted to cry.

"All right, girls. Return to your desk. You have another half hour. I would suggest you study your history."

Helen sighed. She had no idea how to handle this situation. Ordinarily, she'd take the matter up with P.J., but the director had gone to New Orleans to meet with a family who was interested in the school for their son. Since she had family of her own there, P.J. had decided to stay and visit, so she wouldn't be back for at least a week. If Helen couldn't get the situation under control, she'd have to bring it to Trent Quincy's attention.

Patrick looked around the dining room table. Although normal conversation went on amidst the teachers and students, the tension in the room was tangible. He glanced at Helen, who ate her breakfast in silence, only looking up when someone spoke directly to her.

Molly had run to him when she saw him in the foyer and thrown her arms around him. But instead of the bubbling over happiness that usually permeated her greeting, she'd burst into tears. She'd said she was crying because she was happy to see him, but that didn't ring true or even make sense.

Helen left the dining room while he was speaking with Howard. When he stepped into the foyer, he found her waiting for him. "Mr. Flannigan, could I have a word with you?"

"Yes, of course. I was going to ask you the same thing." He motioned toward the front porch. "Shall we go outside?"

"Yes, that's fine."

They'd just seated themselves when Molly charged out the door. "Papa!"

"He stood and motioned to his daughter. "I'm over here, Molly."

"I didn't know where you were." She twisted her hands together.

"Well, as you can see, here I am." He smiled. "I need a moment with Miss Edwards then we'll go for a drive, all right?"

Molly sent Helen an imploring glance then she turned to her father. "Can't I stay here with you?"

He gave her a puzzled look then glanced at Helen. "Does someone want to tell me what's going on?"

"I think Molly should answer that." Helen looked at Molly. "Do you want to tell your father what's wrong, since you won't tell me?"

Molly stood breathing hard. She moistened her lips and darted a glance toward the front door. "Papa, can we go somewhere? Just you and me, so I can tell you?"

He frowned and sent a questioning glance toward Helen.

Helen nodded. "I think that's a good idea, Patrick. You and I can talk later."

Molly grabbed his hand. "Hurry, Papa. Let's go now."

As the carriage drove away, Helen sank back into the wicker rocker. She sent up a prayer that Molly would open up to Patrick and get her fears out into the open.

The front door flew open and Margaret stepped out on the porch. She spotted Helen. "Oh, Miss Edwards. You startled me." She glanced around. "Have you seen Molly?"

"Yes, you just missed her, dear. She went for a drive with her father." Helen peered at the girl to see her reaction.

Margaret's face paled. "Oh. Well, I'd better go back inside."

"Why don't you sit and visit with me for a while?"

"Oh, thank you, but I need to go inside. I have things to do."

"Nevertheless, I'd like for you to stay. I think we need to have a little talk."

"Oh, very well." She flounced over and sat on the cushioned sofa.

"How was practice yesterday?" Helen rocked slowly back and forth.

"Why, it went very well." She threw an impatient look in Helen's direction.

"You have a lovely voice," Helen said. "Good enough for the lead part."

A pleased look washed over Margaret's face. "Yes. I always had the lead parts at my other school."

"Did you now?" She rocked steadily. "I was surprised when Lily Ann withdrew from the cantata. She has a lovely voice as well."

"Does she?" Margaret tossed her curls. "But she's just a little girl. She shouldn't have the lead anyway."

"Hmmm. You think not?" Helen stopped her chair. "Do you have any idea what's wrong with Molly and Trudy? They're not acting like themselves lately."

"No. They seem okay to me. Where did you say Molly and her father went?"

"Just for a drive." Helen paused before going on. "I believe Molly had something she wished to talk to her father about. Something important I believe."

Panic crossed the girl's face.

"Margaret, perhaps there's something you'd like to tell me before they get back."

"No. Why would you think that?" The panic—if indeed Helen hadn't been imagining it—was smoothed over by Margaret's usual sweet expression.

Chapter 10

Trent shook his head, looking almost dazed. "It appears the new student, that angelic appearing little girl, has been terrorizing other children."

Helen flinched at the word *terrorizing*. What in the world had Margaret done? When Patrick and Molly had gotten back from their drive, his face had been set like stone. He'd asked Virgie to please send for Trent Quincy, since the director wasn't there.

Helen had paced the foyer while Patrick, Trent, Molly, and Trudy had been closeted in the director's office for fifteen minutes. Finally, Trent had opened the door and asked Helen to step inside.

She glanced at Molly and Trudy, who sat huddled up together next to Patrick on the small sofa. "Are you girls all right?"

Molly nodded. "Yes, Miss Edwards."

It was the first time Molly had spoken to her in days and she breathed a sigh of relief.

Trent stepped to the door and motioned to someone. A moment later, Virgie appeared.

"Virgie, would you please take Molly and Trudy to the kitchen and get them a glass of milk or something? That is"—he turned with a questioning glance at Patrick—"if it's all right with Mr. Flannigan."

"Yes, but please keep them away from the other children for now, Virgie." Patrick brushed the hair back from Molly's face. "You don't mind going with Miz Virgie, do you?"

Molly shook her head, and the girls stood and followed Virgie from the room. As soon as the door shut behind them, Helen jumped up. "Will someone please tell me what is going on? What has Margaret done?"

Patrick rose, too, and stood by the empty fireplace. "It seems, since the day she arrived, the young lady has been controlling both Molly and Trudy."

"Yes, I was afraid it was something like that. But how did she manage? Trudy is rather timid, but Molly is not a weak-willed girl."

"It seems she threatened if they didn't do everything she told them, she'd hurt Lily Ann."

Helen's stomach knotted. "But surely they wouldn't believe her? Why in the world didn't they tell someone?"

"Apparently she's a very persuasive young lady. She told them poppycock stories of atrocities she'd performed at her former school." Trent's lips clamped together and his face blazed with anger. "Of course, the stories were totally untrue. I spoke to the director of her former school before I approved her enrollment here. According to him, she'd been a model student."

"I wonder... ." Helen frowned. "Oh, not about the atrocities. I'm sure the director would have known if that were true. But she may not have been the model student he thought."

"What do you mean?" Patrick asked.

"I mean, bullies aren't always found out, because their victims don't usually tell." She bit her lip. "Molly and her father are close. She knew he'd believe her and she trusted him to make things right. But that's not always the case."

Trent nodded. "I see what you mean. Well, I suppose I need to contact her parents. We can't have a child here that terrorizes the other students."

That word again. "I wouldn't exactly call it terrorizing. More like bullying. But she must be troubled to do such a thing."

Patrick took a deep breath. "Are you suggesting she be allowed to stay?"

"No. It's not my place to do that. But I think she should have a chance to defend herself."

"Molly wouldn't lie about it!" Patrick protested. "I thought you knew her better than that."

"Of course I do." She laid her hand on his arm and then quickly dropped it. What had possessed her to do something so intimate? "But Margaret needs to speak for herself."

"Helen's right." Trent strode to the door and pulled a bell cord. When Sissy appeared, he instructed her to escort Margaret to the office.

The fear in Margaret's eyes and the ghastly paleness of her face as she walked into the room struck a chord of sympathy in Helen.

"Hello, Margaret." Trent motioned to a chair he'd placed in the middle of the room facing him, Patrick, and Helen. She sat on the edge of the seat and swallowed audibly.

"Margaret, it has come to our attention that you've been

bullying some of the other students." Trent tapped his fingers on his knee.

"No, I haven't," the child's voice shrilled.

"Young lady, it would be better to tell the truth. Lies always get found out in the end." After he'd spoken, Patrick sent Trent an apologetic glance.

She caught her bottom lip between her teeth, and a frown creased her forehead as her eyes filled with tears.

Helen's heart hurt for the child. What could have caused her to behave in such a way?

"I'm sorry." Margaret's whisper was almost inaudible.

Trent's expression softened. "Margaret, everyone does things at times they regret. I sincerely hope that's what you mean and that you aren't merely sorry you got caught."

A crimson blush rushed across her face, and she licked her lips. "I…I don't know. I'm just sorry. What are you going to do to me?"

Trent looked at the girl for a moment. "Why did you threaten Molly and Trudy and tell them untrue stories about your actions at your last school?"

"I don't know." She pressed her lips together and her breathing quickened.

Trent threw a helpless glance toward Helen. Apparently he'd never dealt with a serious disciplinary problem before. He turned his attention back to the girl. "I'm sorry. I can't accept that as an answer. Until we get to the bottom of this, you're confined to your room. I will, of course, notify your parents of your behavior."

Panic crossed Margaret's face and her hands tightened into a fist.

"That will be all for now. You're dismissed to your room."

"Please don't…" Margaret heaved a sigh. "Yes, sir."

After the door closed behind her, Helen immediately

turned to Trent. "Would you mind if I talk to Margaret and try to get to the bottom of this?"

"By all means." Trent took a handkerchief from his pocket and dabbed his forehead. "Let me know if you have any success."

Helen nodded and glanced at Patrick. "I know you're angry because of what she did to Molly, but try not to judge her too harshly until we find out more."

He nodded. "I'll try. After all, she's only a child. I wish you success."

Helen set the dinner tray on a small table outside Margaret's room, tapped lightly before opening the door, and walked in.

Margaret looked up from the window seat. "Miss Edwards. You brought my supper?"

Helen smiled. "You didn't think we'd let you go hungry, did you?" She glanced around and spotted a table in the corner. "Why don't you move that table over here for your tray and I'll visit with you while you eat."

Margaret jumped up and hurried to do as instructed. When she was seated again, she laid the snowy white napkin across her lap and lifted the dome lid from her plate. "Oh, ham and sweet potatoes. My favorite."

"Yes, and that little covered dish contains peach cobbler." She moved a glass of milk closer to Margaret. "Cook thought you'd like the cobbler."

Margaret put down her knife and fork and turned wide eyes upon Helen. "Why is everyone being so nice to me after what I've done?"

"Well, first of all, very few people know the details, and besides, we care about you, Margaret. And I, for one, would like to help, if you'll let me." She motioned to the tray. "Why don't you eat before your food gets cold? We can talk afterward."

Margaret ate slowly, finally pushing the tray away. She turned to Helen. "What do you want me to say?"

Surprised, Helen said, "The truth, of course. I'd like to know why you threatened to hurt Lily. Why you ordered the girls not to talk to me, and what this all has to do with Lily Ann. Because it does have something to do with her, doesn't it?"

Margaret's eyes widened and she ducked her head. "I always have the lead."

A knot formed in Helen's stomach. "What do you mean?"

"You see, my mother is very proud of my voice and she expects me to have the lead. Always." She bit her lip.

"But, sweetheart, I'm sure your mother understands that sometimes that's not going to happen. Lily Ann has a lovely voice, too. And she already had the part before you arrived."

"But I want my mother to be proud of me." Tears swam in her blue eyes and began to run down her cheeks. "She's so good at everything and all I can do is sing."

Helen closed her eyes for a moment and took a deep breath. "How did you get Lily Ann to withdraw from the cantata, Margaret?"

Shame washed over the child's face. "I—I..."

"Please tell me."

"I told her if she didn't, I would trip Mrs. Quincy and make her lose the baby."

Waves of nausea and shock washed over Helen. "You would have done that?"

"No, no,"—sobs broke out from Margaret—"no, I wouldn't have. Not really."

"But Lily Ann thought you would, so she did what you wanted."

"Yes." Margaret's voice broke as sob after sob racked her body.

"There's more, isn't there?" Helen laid her hand on Margaret's shoulder. "You might as well tell me all of it."

"I made Lily Ann promise not to tell anyone. But Trudy saw me talking to her, saw her crying. She told Molly, and they came and told me to leave Lily Ann alone."

"And that's when you threatened them?"

"Uh-huh. I was afraid they'd tell. So I told them they had to stay away from Lily Ann and if they told anyone about any of it, I'd hurt her." By now she seemed bent on telling all. "I made some stories up so they'd believe that I'd really do mean things.

"But why wouldn't they speak to me?"

"I was mad because you liked Molly so much." She gulped. "I guess that was just being mean. I told them they couldn't talk to you."

The memory of the episode in the classroom with Trudy and Molly ran through Helen's mind. "But you forgot to tell them not to sign."

"Miss Edwards. I don't know what got into me. I never did anything like this before. I promise."

"I believe you, Margaret." Helen reached over and tucked a stray hair back in the girl's ribbon. "Jealousy can be ugly and vicious. Just as other sins."

At the word *sin*, Margaret gasped. "I didn't know I was sinning. Is God mad at me?"

"Margaret, God loves us and sent Jesus to pay the price for our sins." She looked directly at the girl. "Have you accepted Jesus as your savior?"

Margaret nodded with tears flooding down her cheeks.

"Yes, ma'am. But I forgot about Him for a while. Does that mean I'm not a Christian anymore?"

Helen swallowed past the lump that formed in her throat. "Sweetheart, 1 John 1:9 tells us 'if we confess our sins, he is faithful and just to forgive us our sins, and to cleanse us from all unrighteousness.'"

"Can I do that now?" She slipped off the window seat and knelt by her bed. In a few minutes she rose. "I know He forgave me. But I have to tell Molly and Trudy and Lily Ann I'm sorry and ask them to forgive me, too."

"I'm sure they will, Margaret." Helen stood and picked up the tray. "If you need me for anything, ring for Sissy and she'll come get me."

"Thank you, Miss Edwards." Margaret opened the door for her. "I know how much you care for Molly. Thank you for not being mad at me."

Helen took the tray to the kitchen then went to have her own supper. Trudy and Lily Ann were subdued but the tension was gone. Molly had gone to the hotel to have supper with her father. Afterward, Helen stepped outside and sat, all the events of the day rushing through her mind. Trent would speak to Lily Ann and her parents after church on Sunday, but Helen needed to tell him what Margaret had confessed. Abigail also needed to know because of the situation with the cantata.

The sound of horse hooves and the jingle of the harness drifted up the lane and the carriage came into sight.

The welcome sound of Molly's giggle rang out. Patrick helped her down from the carriage. "Good night, Papa." She ran up the steps and went inside without seeing Helen.

"It sounds like we have our happy girl back."

Patrick started. "Helen. I didn't see you." He came up the steps and onto the porch then sat in the chair next to her.

Leaning back, he took a deep breath. "What a day."

"Yes, it was indeed." Helen smiled. "Margaret confessed to everything."

Relief crossed his face. "Why did she do those things?"

"Well, the surface reason, if you can believe this, is that she wanted to sing the lead in the cantata." Helen frowned. "But I believe there's a deeper reason behind it all."

"Well, I hate to see any child punished, but that young lady needs to learn a lesson so it doesn't happen again."

"Yes, of course she does. But I think she's truly sorry. We had a talk before supper."

Helen told him everything that had transpired with Margaret. "I believe she was sincere, Patrick."

He nodded. "I hope so. What action do you think Trent will take?"

"I don't know. He's planning to speak to her parents as soon as possible. But for now, she's confined to her room, except for school."

"I'm thankful Molly told me about it. There's no telling how long it would have gone on or what course it would have taken next."

Helen nodded. "Or it may not have lasted much longer. The fact that she caved in and confessed everything so readily makes me think her conscience was hurting her already."

He smiled and touched her hand. "You have a sweet soul, Helen Edwards. You always seem to see the good in people."

She blushed. "Thank you, Patrick. I'm afraid I'm not quite as good-hearted as you think. I struggle with ill thoughts toward people just as everyone does. It's a process, I guess. By God's grace, we grow in character."

"Yes, but some of us have prettier characters than others. I don't know anyone I'd rather spend time with." He touched her cheek. "There, I've embarrassed you. I didn't mean to do that."

"You didn't embarrass me." She turned her head. "Well, perhaps just a little. I enjoy your company, too."

"Helen."

Her pulse quickened as he looked deeply into her eyes. She caught her breath. She wasn't ready for this. Besides, nothing had changed. His life was in Atlanta. Hers was here. She jumped up. "I really need to check on Margaret. I'll see you at church in the morning."

Without giving him a chance to say anything more, she hurried inside.

Chapter 11

The rustle of starched dresses and scuffling of shoes joined the muffled laughter and conversation of neighbors and friends who hadn't seen one another for a week.

Helen helped usher the children to their seats on the long pews. She stepped into the row, but before she could sit, she felt a hand on her elbow. Her heart gave a little jump as she looked up into Patrick's smiling face.

She moved over so Molly could sit beside her with Patrick on the end. Flashing them both a smile, Helen straightened her spine and looked forward to where Silas Monroe, the song leader of the day, stood behind the pulpit, fanning through the pages of the hymnal.

Silas cleared his throat loudly, and the congregation gave him their attention. "Good morning, brothers and sisters. It's nice to see you all here on this fine, sunshiny Lord's day. The first song we're gonna sing reflects that nicely. Turn to page 47."

Helen knew the lovely gospel song by heart, and she sang along with the other raised voices.

Oh there's sunshine, blessed sunshine,
When the peaceful, happy moments roll;
When Jesus shows His smiling face,
There is sunshine in the soul.

To be honest, she wasn't feeling all that sunshiny this morning. The situation with Margaret still hung over them. Dr. Trent had decided to leave the matter in the director's hands since she was expected back the next day. So, until then, the girl was confined to her room except to attend church services.

But that wasn't the only thing weighing on her. She couldn't deny to herself any longer that her feelings for Patrick had grown beyond friendship. And if his actions were any indication, he felt the same toward her. She'd struggled most of the night with the conflict in her heart. Should she take the chance on falling in love and having to leave the school and the children who meant so much to her? If not, then could she harden her heart toward Patrick and prevent that from happening?

She started at a tug on her sleeve and realized everyone had stood. She gave Molly a smile and stood, her face blazing.

Patrick threw her a questioning lift of an eyebrow, and she pretended not to see but focused on the hymnal as they sang the last verse.

Reverend Shepherd's message was on hearing God's voice. Helen listened intently. How could she know she was doing God's will? Obviously His Word was His will, but some things couldn't be found in the Bible. What about finding God's will when the choices were both good ones? How did one know?

The reverend spoke of letting God guide you, of God's still, small voice and inner peace, but Helen couldn't quite wrap her mind around what he was saying. Of course, there had been times when she knew in her heart that she was or was not making a right decision. But many times, she continued to struggle. She sighed. One thing she was sure of—God's Word was truth and if she didn't understand then it wasn't God's fault.

As she stepped outside, the noonday sun hit her full in the face. Oh dear, a hot day for the beginning of April.

After she'd shaken Reverend Shepherd's hand, she started to walk toward the wagon.

"Helen."

She turned at the sound of Patrick's voice to find him and Molly with eager looks on their faces.

"Molly and I would be pleased if you'd go to dinner at the hotel with us." He ran his fingers around the brim of his hat and gave her a hopeful smile.

"I'm sorry. I'm Margaret's monitor today. I can't leave the school." Gazing on their disappointed faces, she added, "But I wish I could accept your offer."

"Then perhaps we can go for a walk later."

"Perhaps. As long as we don't go far."

Helen watched them drive away and turned to help get the younger children into the wagon. Disappointment and relief battled inside her.

At the school, Selma had prepared a dinner of pork chops, sweet potatoes, stuffing, glazed carrots, and all the home-canned condiments for which she was famous. Helen barely tasted the delicious meal. She did, however, drink several glasses of sweet tea and had a small slice of caramel pecan cake. In spite of everything, she felt better afterward. She chuckled to herself. Perhaps sugar was a medicine.

After the girls had helped clear the table, Helen escorted Margaret to her room.

"Do I have to stay here all day again today? I need some air. Can't you take me outside for a little while?" She gave Helen a pleading look.

One thing that didn't work with Helen was cajoling. She'd been teaching far too long for that to sway her. "I'm very sorry, dear, but Dr. Trent was quite clear. Besides, you've just had a nice drive in the fresh air to the church and back."

Margaret sighed and flounced over to the window seat. "Oh all right. I know I deserve it."

"Miss Wellington will arrive tomorrow, dear." Just saying the words brought relief to Helen. P.J. could get on her nerves sometimes, but there was no denying that things went much more smoothly when she was here. "Then we'll get this whole thing straightened out."

"What do you think she'll do to me, Miss Edwards?" The girl's voice held a niggling of fear.

"She'll be fair. That's all I can say for certain." Helen gave an emphatic nod. "Miss Wellington is always fair."

Margaret sighed. "Any punishment she can think of would be fair. What I did wasn't nice at all."

Helen wished she could have allowed Margaret to speak to Molly, Trudy, and Lily Ann. Once Margaret made things right with them, things would be better. But without permission from Dr. Trent, who wasn't at church this morning, Helen couldn't give her permission.

"No, it wasn't nice at all, but God has forgiven you and I know the girls will, too. Would you like for me to bring you some more books?"

"No, thank you." Margaret gave her a pensive look. "I believe I'll write in my diary and draw a little."

"I'm very happy you have a diary. I've kept one since I was nine years old. And I'd love to see your drawings one day, if you wouldn't mind."

"I guess that would be all right." She stood and lifted the lid of the window seat.

Helen left and went to her own room. *Dear God, please let this work out for everyone's good.*

Patrick tried to focus on Molly, but his mind kept drifting to Helen. Had she seemed a little distant today?

"Papa, did you hear what I said?" Molly put her fork on her plate and frowned.

"What? Oh, Molly, I'm so sorry. I'm a little distracted today." He took a drink of tea.

She gave him a forgiving smile. "It's all right, Papa. I was just wondering if you think you'll ever get married again."

He coughed as the sweet tea went down wrong. He grabbed a napkin as he continued to cough while Molly pounded him on the back.

When he caught his breath again, he looked at Molly. "Why did you ask that?"

"Oh, I don't know. You're not really old, you know. And Trudy said you'd probably want to get married again someday."

"Oh she did, did she? What do you think of the idea?"

She looked up at the ceiling with a wise expression on her face. "Oh, I think it would depend on who you wanted to marry. She'd have to be nice and like children. Especially me."

He nodded. "Yes, I can see that would be a necessary requirement. Did you have someone in mind?"

She grabbed her fork and took a bite of apple pie. After swallowing, she nodded. "Miss Edwards is nice and she's not married yet. It would be a shame if she had to be an old maid all her life."

He pressed his lips together to hide a grin. "I suppose she seems old to you?"

"Well, sort of. But we wouldn't want some silly young girl to live with us, would we?"

"No, I guess not." He shook his head. The things the child came up with. "But perhaps Miss Edwards wouldn't like to be married to me."

Molly's lips curled up in a smile. "I think she likes you."

A pleasant jolt ran through him. "Why do you think so?"

"Oh, Papa," she rolled her eyes and signed, "I'm not a baby. I see how she looks at you."

"How?" He held his breath.

"The same way you look at her when you don't think anyone sees you." She giggled.

Startled, he sent her an anxious glance. "You're imagining things."

She cut a glance his way and licked her fork. "I don't think so."

Patrick laughed. "Finish your pie, Miss See-all and Know-all. We need to get back to the school."

Well, it seemed he had his daughter's approval. Too bad it wasn't a practical idea.

As they drove out of town, she turned to him. "So are you going to?"

"Am I going to what, angel?"

An exaggerated sigh escaped her lips. "Propose marriage to Miss Edwards."

"Honey, it's not that simple. I couldn't ask Helen to give

up the teaching position she loves. And my shop and our home are in Atlanta."

"Oh, that's no problem." She brushed a piece of lint off her skirt. "Move the shop here."

Helen caught herself glancing out the door again. She simply had to stop that. They'd be here when they got here. And she had to stop caring. She spun on her heel and headed for the stairs. Perhaps she should go find something to work on.

In her room, she sat in the rocker by her window and picked up the pillowcase she was embroidering. After stabbing at the fabric and sticking her finger for the third time, she sighed. Maybe she'd take her embroidery out on the porch and work in the fresh air.

She stood and carried the pillowcase with her downstairs. The murmur of voices drifted from the parlor. She stepped to the parlor door and looked inside. Virgie and Felicity sat in matching rockers working on costumes.

"Mind if I join you?"

"You come right on in here and sit yourself down." Virgie motioned to a chair across from her. "There be a nice cool breeze coming through the window."

Helen grinned. What Virgie considered a nice cool breeze barely moved the lace curtain. But then, Virgie had lived in Georgia all her life.

After Helen was seated, she picked up a fan and moved it back and forth. "It feels like summer, already."

"Uh uh, baby girl," Virgie shook her head, "you ought to know better than that. How many years you been here?"

"You're right. Come July, this would feel cool." Helen smoothed the pillowcase and began pulling the pale pink thread through the material to form a flower petal.

"How that Margaret girl doing up there shut up in her room?"

"She's lonely, I think, but she'll be okay."

"Give her plenty of time to think about her ways." Virgie's soft voice soothed Helen's mind, relaxing her.

"I expect you're right," Felicity agreed. "She'll think twice before she pulls a trick like that again."

Helen held up her embroidery and peered at one of the stitches. Was it a little crooked? She pulled it out and redid it. "I believe she's truly sorry. And who knows the real root cause for what she did?"

Virgie gave her an approving smile. "I expect you'll be finding out."

"I certainly hope to." She wondered if there was any basis to Margaret's fear of her mother's disapproval. She had only spoken with the parents for a few moments when they brought Margaret to the school. The lady had seemed very nice, but of course, looks could be deceiving.

Virgie nodded. "How are the childrun liking their new classrooms?"

Helen threw her a look of thanks for changing the subject. "They are settling in very nicely. And they love the auditorium. It echoes."

Virgie gave a soft chuckle. "I expect it does. Big, old, hollow room like that. When it gets filled up with chairs and people, it won't echo so much."

Helen glanced at the green velvet Felicity was fashioning into knee length breeches. She wondered which lady of the Quincy family had worn it and to what occasion.

The sound of a carriage out front drew her attention, and she glanced toward the door then quickly back. Virgie sent her a knowing smile.

"What?"

"I didn't say anything." But Virgie's smile grew bigger.

Felicity giggled. "Anyone can see you and Mr. Flannigan like each other."

Helen's face flamed. "Of course we like each other. As friends. Nothing else," she snapped.

Felicity nodded. "If you say so."

The screen door squeaked open and Helen shushed her. "Be quiet. He'll hear you."

"All right. All right." Felicity pressed her lips together and made a motion as if she were buttoning them.

"Oh, you."

"Bye, Papa, I'll see you in a little while." Molly's voice rang out. "Don't forget what we talked about."

Her shoes tapped across the foyer and up the stairs.

"Someone better go see if that man need something. He just standing in the foyer."

Helen stood and laid her embroidery on the chair. "Oh, all right. I'll go."

Patrick stood in the foyer looking around helplessly. Relief crossed his face when she stepped out of the parlor.

"I wasn't sure where to find you," he said.

"Oh, were you looking for me?"

"Yes, we talked earlier about going for a walk? I wondered if you're still interested."

"I think that would be fine. Let me put my sewing away."

She stepped into the parlor and picked up her embroidery. "I'm going to look in on Margaret then go for a walk."

Felicity grinned. "I can check on Margaret for you."

"No, thank you. I need to put my sewing away, anyway. And get that smug look off your face, Felicity. We're just friends."

"If you say so."

Helen shook her head and went upstairs. Margaret was busy writing in her diary and didn't need anything, so Helen went to her room to put her things away. She straightened her dress and patted her hair. Should she change her blouse? No, of course not. The one she was wearing was just fine even though rather plain.

She took a deep breath and changed into a pretty blue blouse with a lace-trimmed collar. She might as well look nice if she was going to stroll down the lane. After all, it was Sunday afternoon. You never knew who would come to visit. *Oh, stop it, Helen,* she scolded herself. *You want to look nice for Patrick.*

She lifted her chin and went downstairs.

Chapter 12

The fragrance of magnolia blossoms saturated the air as Helen and Patrick strolled down the lane. The peach trees were just starting to blossom as well. Helen inhaled deeply. One of the things she loved most about Georgia. The fragrance from early spring and throughout the summer was almost enough to offset the heavy, humid heat, which was already making its discomfort known.

They stopped just before the gate and sat on the bench beneath the old live oak tree.

"It's so beautiful here in the spring." Helen glanced around. "Sometimes I sit here and imagine the Quincy family and their friends before the War. I can almost see them strolling on the lawns and gardens, the ladies in their wide hoopskirts and the men in their ruffled shirts."

Patrick grinned. "I'd say those ruffled shirts and hoopskirts weren't too comfortable in the summer time."

Helen smiled. "Probably not. The things we put up with for fashion."

"So you think you'd like to have lived in that period of time?" He pulled a piece of grass and tapped it against his palm.

"Heavens, no! I could never have tolerated slavery. It must have been horrible for the slaves." A shudder went through her.

Patrick sighed. "Yes, it must have been. I wonder if their owners realized that."

"Some of them, perhaps. But I imagine, for those who were born and raised in that society, it was just part of life. It was the way things were."

"Are any of the servants here former slaves?"

Helen bit her lip and sadness washed over her face. She nodded. "Virgie and Albert. But I believe they were quite young when the late Mrs. Quincy set all the family slaves free."

"Set them free?"

"Yes, well before the War. As I understand it, her husband left everything to her when he passed away." Admiration for the brave woman washed over her as it did every time she thought about it. "She freed all the slaves and gave them each land and a cabin. The ones who wanted to continue to work for her received salaries. Most of the blacks around here are descendants of those same slaves."

Patrick shook his head. "You don't hear too many stories like that. She must have been a fine woman."

"Yes, but probably not too popular with her neighbors afterward."

A carriage came around the bend and stopped at the gate. The driver got down and opened it.

"Look. It's P.J. We weren't expecting her until tomorrow." Helen waved as the carriage rolled by them.

Patrick stood and tipped his hat as the director waved back then motioned for them to follow. "That's good. Perhaps we can get this thing with Margaret settled and I won't need to stay over."

Disappointment tugged at Helen, but she managed to keep a pleasant expression on her face.

"Not that I'm eager to go," Patrick said, "but I have a business to run."

"Yes, of course." And there it was again, glaring in Helen's face and bursting her enjoyment of the afternoon. His life was in Atlanta; hers was here. "I suppose we'd better get back to the house to welcome her back."

When they entered the house, the foyer was teeming with excited children surrounding P.J., each attempting to tell her hello. Helen grinned. P.J. could be firm in her speech sometimes, but she had a heart of gold and the children knew it.

Felicity and Howard finally managed to round the younger children up and take them to the mudroom to wash up for supper. The older students trailed behind. Enticing aromas drifted out the door from the kitchen area.

P.J. gave a little moan of delight. "I have sorely missed Selma's cooking."

"Miz Wellington, Selma is one right good cook." Virgie believed in giving credit where credit was due and never mentioned that she'd taught Cook everything she knew.

"Now, let me go freshen up. Miss Edwards, Miss Wilson, and Mr. Waverly, I'd like to see the three of you in my office after supper, if you please." She grew suddenly serious. "I need you to explain to me about the incident with our new student."

"How in the world did you find out about it?" Charles asked her.

"I received a telegram from Dr. Quincy, but he told me

very little. So I finished my business affairs and took the first train I could get."

"Actually, Helen is the one who knows the details." Charles glanced hopefully from P.J. to Helen. "The rest of us have heard very little of the matter. Perhaps she's the one you need to speak with."

"Very well. Now let me go. I'm hot from the sun, dusty from the train, and famished."

"Wait, Miss Wellington," Helen called after her. "I believe Mr. Flannigan should be included in our conversation. His daughter is involved in this, and he must return to Atlanta tomorrow."

"All right. Mr. Flannigan, too." P.J. fluttered the fingers of one hand over her shoulder without turning around.

Charles and Hannah headed toward the dining room.

Patrick glanced down at Helen. "Thank you for suggesting my presence at your meeting with the director.

"Of course, you should be there." She nodded. "I need to take a tray up to Margaret. I'll see you in a few minutes in the dining room."

Since the children were eating their supper upstairs, the teachers and director and Patrick had the dining room to themselves. As much as Helen loved the students, the supper meal was her favorite of the day. The relaxing, casual conversation of adult friends and colleagues melted away the cares of the day.

She was pleased, if not a little embarrassed, when Patrick seated himself beside her.

Sissy served alone tonight since there were only a few dining. She dished up the soup and filled their glasses with either water or sweet tea then left the room with a soft swish of her skirts.

The main course was a cold chicken dish with vegetables on the side, followed by a rice pudding.

When the meal was over, Helen and Patrick followed P.J. to her office. After Patrick told her what Molly had revealed to him, Helen took over and talked about the meeting with Dr. Trent and Margaret's subsequent confession.

"Dr. Trent confined Margaret to her room until your return." Helen went on to tell her about Margaret's sorrow over what she'd done and her repentance to God. "She desires to apologize to Molly, Trudy, and Lily Ann, but of course, I couldn't give her permission to approach them. I'll leave that up to you."

P.J. stood. "Thank you both. Helen, I'll speak with Margaret tomorrow. I'll also need to talk to the other three girls. And of course, I'll send a wire to Margaret's parents asking them to come. They need to know what's going on. Perhaps they'll have an idea of the root cause of her behavior." She frowned. "They may choose to remove her from the school."

He should have taken the train last night for Atlanta, but until this situation with the girls was cleared up, he simply couldn't leave his daughter here without being nearby. Patrick left the hotel and walked toward the livery. To be honest, he hated the thought of leaving Helen as well.

As he passed the vacant hardware store, he paused and peered through the window. Plenty of space and it appeared to be clean. The niggling of an idea began to form. He did like the rural area. But could he make a living here? He walked on, a wrinkle creasing his forehead as he thought. The thought of moving his business here hadn't even crossed his mind until Molly had suggested it.

He arrived at the livery and the owner called out from behind the counter. "Good morning, Mr. Flannigan. Will you need the carriage today?"

"No, just a horse." He would be making a quick trip to the school to speak to the director and say farewell to Molly and Helen. A horse would be faster.

He took notice of his surroundings as he rode the two miles to the school. Pink, red, white, and violet wild flowers dotted the green grass and many of the magnolias already had velvety white blossoms. It truly was beautiful and peaceful here.

He rode around the building to the barn. Albert glanced up and grinned, "Morning, Mist' Flannigan. A might fine day, wouldn't you say?"

"I sure would, Albert. Love the sunshine."

"Yes, suh. Not a cloud in the sky." He reached for the reins. "You be stayin' long?"

"I'm not sure. It depends on…" He stopped. He supposed he shouldn't be discussing the matter with Albert. Even if he had been with the school forever.

"Depends on what Miz P.J. gonna do 'bout that chile?" He lifted his wrinkled brown hand and pulled a glossy five-pointed leaf off a sweet gum tree and stuck it between his teeth.

Patrick chuckled. "Is there anything that gets past you?" He patted the horse on the rump and turned to go.

"Not much, suh. Not much." Albert's cackle followed Patrick as he walked toward the house.

The foyer was empty except for one of the maids, who knelt beside a small table, polishing the surface with cedar oil. Patrick's nose twitched at the strong aroma.

"Mornin', Mistuh Flannigan." She nodded then turned back to her chore.

Miss Wellington came down the stairs, followed by Margaret. "Ah, Mister Flannigan. I'm glad you're here. She stepped onto the foyer floor and pulled Margaret beside her. "Well, child, here is the first one I believe you need to speak to."

Margaret's face was pale and tear-streaked. She lifted her eyes and looked at Patrick. Her lips quivered. "Mr. Flannigan, I am so sorry for what I did. Truly I am."

Patrick couldn't help but notice that Margaret's demeanor was much different from when he'd seen her last. Somehow she appeared older than her twelve years, as though she'd left childishness behind. Whereas her sorrow two days before was obviously more from getting caught, her countenance now held true repentance, just as Helen had said.

He reached out and took her hand. "I accept your apology, Margaret. I don't think you'll ever do anything like that again and I forgive you."

Her indrawn sob was followed by a torrent of tears. "Thank you, sir."

Patrick squeezed her hand before gently letting go. He glanced at Miss Wellington, who had a tender but firm look on her face.

The maid stood and with a little curtsy, retreated into the kitchen area. Miss Wellington stepped over to the bell cord and gave a tug.

A moment later, one of the older maids appeared. "Yes, ma'am?"

"Sally May, please fetch Molly and Trudy from Miss Wilson's class and Lily Ann from Miss Edwards's and ask them to come to my office. And tell both teachers I won't keep them long."

Sally May headed up the stairs and Miss Wellington turned to Patrick. "Mr. Flannigan, I'm having a meeting later today with the teachers. You are welcome to stay and join us if you can. If you need to get back to Atlanta,

I assure you there will not be a repeat of this unfortunate incident."

Patrick glanced at Margaret, who said, "I promise, sir. I only hope Molly and Trudy will still want to be my friends. But I won't blame them if they don't."

"I believe you, Margaret." He turned to the director. "If you don't mind, I'll stay for the midday meal so I can say farewell to the teachers."

A hint of a smile graced Miss Wellington's lips and her eyes danced. "Absolutely you should stay. I'm sure the *teachers* will want to say good-bye to you as well."

At the emphasis on teachers, a hint of suspicion bit at Patrick and he peered at the director. However, her face was composed and her eyes as well. Perhaps he'd imagined the teasing tone in her voice."

Helen stood on the porch watching Patrick ride away on the chestnut mare. His back was straight and the muscles in his shirt sleeves tightened over his biceps. A shiver ran across her shoulders as she imagined a knight of old on his trusted steed. A laugh escaped her lips. *Really, Helen Edwards. Get a grip on yourself and stop acting like a love-struck girl.*

She turned and went inside.

Virgie had just come out of the dining room, presumably inspecting it to make sure it was in perfect shape after the midday meal. She smiled at Helen. "You like that red-headed Irishman, now, don't you?"

Helen felt her face flame. Apparently Felicity wasn't the only one who'd uncovered her secret. "He's a very nice man. Of course I like him."

"Umm. Hmm. I think it's more than his nice ways you like."

Helen laughed. "All right, Virgie. I do like Patrick. But there's no sense in even thinking about it."

"And why's that? Can't you see the way that man look at you, honey?"

Helen sighed. She couldn't deny that. "But it's hopeless. His business is in Atlanta and I can't leave the school."

Surprise crossed the soft brown face. "Why you think that?"

"Why, because I'm needed here. Especially now that the school is growing. More students will be enrolling next year." What was Virgie thinking?

"Land sake, child." Virgie touched her cheek. "You ain't the only one who can teach these young'uns. I expect there be a line of young gals just waiting for the chance."

Shock ran through Helen. How could Virgie say she wasn't needed? She swallowed past the sudden lump in her throat. "I need to grade some papers, Virgie. I'll see you at supper."

She rushed upstairs and into her empty classroom, happy that the children were in other classes this hour. It would be different next year. There would be so many they'd have to divide up the classes into groups.

She sat and placed her face in her hands. Could Virgie be right? Was she really not needed here? She knew there were other teachers who were just as qualified as she to teach deaf children, but she'd been working hard to learn braille so she could help Lily Ann. Now that Abigail was expecting a baby, it would be out of the question for her to do it as she'd planned.

Mixed emotions ran through her. She could marry Patrick, if he asked. But how could she bear to be away from these children? She'd taught some of them for years.

Well, he likely wasn't going to ask anyway. So why get herself all stirred up over nothing. But what if he did?

Could she bring herself to go away? Even if there were other qualified teachers would they love these precious children the way she did?

Helen sighed. The idea was too fresh in her mind. She wouldn't think about it right now. Besides, she had work to do.

Chapter 13

P.J. looked exhausted. Helen sympathized. The director had been gone for nearly a week and then returned to a problem that required a great deal of wisdom to resolve. Both windows in the office were open, but no air circulated and the late afternoon heat was oppressive. Helen's arms, in elbow length sleeves, were too warm and her forearm clung to the leather chair's arm. The other teachers looked just as uncomfortable.

"I won't keep you long. I know you have things to do before supper." P.J. picked up a cardboard fan from her desk and moved it rapidly back and forth then returned it to its resting place. "I'm sure you're all aware of the incident with Margaret."

Charles cleared his throat. "Miss Wilson and I only know there was a problem concerning Margaret and some of the other children."

Hannah nodded. "All I really know is that Margaret is confined to her room."

P.J. nodded. "Margaret has been bullying three of the other girls. Not physically, but rather psychologically. I believe the girl is truly sorry for what she's done. She has even repented to God and apologized to the girls and to one of the parents."

"Well, that's good." Charles seemed a little confused. "Will she be returning to class soon?"

P.J. sighed and picked up the fan. She tapped it against the desk then laid it back down. "I'll go into Mimosa Junction in the morning and send a telegram to her parents. They need to know about this. Perhaps they'll have an idea of the root cause of her behavior.

"In the meantime, I would like to allow Margaret to return to her regular class schedule and take her meals in the dining room. As I said, she's repented of her actions and I don't believe we'll have any more trouble on that line. The other three girls have assured me they haven't discussed this with the other children so there shouldn't be any problem. I did, however, want you to be aware of the situation. Some disciplinary action is needed, so she will not be allowed to go outside during recess or after school until I hear from her parents. I would appreciate it if one or more of you would volunteer to take her outside for an hour of exercise and fresh air once a day."

Helen was about to offer to do it when Hannah spoke up. "I'd be happy to do that, Miss Wellington."

"Thank you, Miss Wilson. I was hoping you would volunteer." She smiled. "I know you have a younger sister near Margaret's age. And you're not that much older yourself." She chuckled.

Hannah blushed. "Yes, ma'am. I'm happy to do it."

Helen flinched. But P.J. was right. Margaret probably

needed someone young to help her through this time. Hannah Wilson was all of twenty-one. At thirty-two, Helen sometimes felt ancient. Most of the girls she'd gone to school with had been married for years and had children. *My, how time passed.*

She sighed. She needed to snap out of this melancholy before she started feeling sorry for herself. She didn't regret the years she'd spent teaching. She loved her work and the students. Still, she had to admit, sometimes her heart longed for a family of her own. A sudden picture of Molly's deep blue eyes and Patrick's sea green ones smiling at her in much the same way appeared in her mind.

She jumped up. "Yes, that's a wonderful idea, Hannah. And now, if we're finished, I have some essays to grade before I go to bed."

A loud boom reverberated through the room followed by a rolling of thunder that lasted several minutes. Helen placed her hand on her chest and gave a shaky laugh. "Whew! That was close."

"It sure was," Hannah said between gasps of breath.

Charles laughed. "Well, we need rain to cool things off a bit. Don't let a little thunder scare you, ladies."

P.J. frowned. "That first one sounded like something was hit."

Someone pounded on the door and Albert burst in. "Miz Wellington. The live oak tree by the gate been hit. It split plumb in two."

Within moments, they followed Albert down the lane. Half the tree lay across the lane, its shiny green leaves scattered everywhere. The bench she'd sat on with Patrick the day before was hidden beneath, more than likely shattered.

"Oh dear!" P.J. slapped her palm against one cheek. "What a mess."

"Yes, ma'am." Albert stood shaking his head. "It is that.

Reckon I best be gittin' the mules hitched up and yank that thing off the road."

"You need help, Albert," P.J. said. "And don't tell me you don't. Get a couple of the Hedley boys to give you a hand. They can cut the trunk into firewood. When they're finished, send them to my office and I'll pay them for their work."

"Yes'm. If you say so." Albert's face reflected his displeasure and he walked away mumbling. "Could do it myself, though."

Helen grinned at P.J. "I think you've insulted him."

Charles chuckled. "The man thinks he's still a spring chicken. I wonder how old he is, anyway." When no one answered, he gave a wave. "I have some things to do before supper. And I think I smelled apple cobbler when we came through the foyer. I'm famished."

Hannah nodded and followed.

P.J. glanced at Helen. "Do *you* have any idea how old Albert is?"

Helen thought for a moment, doing some mental calculations. "I'm not sure, but he's older than Virgie and she was an adult when old Mrs. Quincy freed the slaves. I'd say Albert is at least in his sixties. Maybe older."

P.J. nodded. "Ten years older than me or more. That settles it. I'm going to talk to Dr. Quincy about hiring another hand to help Albert with the work around here."

"I'm sure Dr. Trent will agree, but Albert's going to throw a fit," Helen said. "Is Margaret to have her supper with the other children tonight? Or should I take her a tray?"

"I think a tray tonight. I need to speak to Felicity and Howard before having her join them again. Also the girls who help out during the supper hour will need to know the rules concerning her discipline."

Another clap of thunder pealed through the air. Helen nearly jumped out of her skin and noticed that P.J. had started as well. Lightning flashed across the darkened sky. Helen grabbed her skirt as the wind whipped it around. Large drops of rain splattered on Helen's skin and on the lane leading to the house.

"Here it comes," P.J. yelled over the noise and took off running to the house.

Helen lifted her skirts and hurried after the director. Maybe the rain would cool things off, either that or make it more hot and humid. Either way, she didn't want to get caught in a downpour.

Patrick sank into his seat just as the storm broke. He'd missed the earlier train, but it had given him a chance to meet with the man who was handling Tom Mill's property and make an appointment to see the building on Saturday.

He still wasn't sure why he'd done it. Why would he want to move a business that had just begun to prosper? Not to mention the fact that he owned a home in Atlanta. Molly might not want to leave the only home she'd known. Although, now that he thought of it, she was the one who'd put the idea of moving to Mimosa Junction into his head.

Well, it wouldn't hurt anything to look at the former hardware store. Just to satisfy his curiosity. Even though he had no real intention of moving from Atlanta, the memory of Helen's small hand on his arm the day before mocked his resolution.

He slid down in the seat and pulled his hat forward to cover his eyes. Maybe he could sleep on the way to Atlanta. Maybe he could escape the sight and scent of Helen while he slept.

* * *

The storm raged outside Helen's window. Clap after clap of thunder shattered the air and rain poured down in torrents. Between the storm and thoughts of Patrick, she'd tossed and turned for the past two hours. Just as she began to drop off to sleep, a flash of lightning lit up her room and she sat straight up. With a sigh of exasperation, she got up. Who could sleep with all this going on?

She poured a glass of water and drank the contents, but it barely made a dent in her thirst. What she really needed was a glass of Selma's lemonade. She knew a pitcher of lemonade was most likely on the kitchen counter.

She slipped her feet into her slippers and threw on her robe, buttoning it up to her neck. Lighting a lamp, she then adjusted the wick. She eased her door open carefully so it wouldn't squeak and tiptoed down the stairs. Was that a light in the parlor?

Helen tiptoed to the half-open door.

Virgie sat with her feet up on a small stool. Blue velvet fabric from one of the old gowns overflowed her lap as she sewed. She glanced up as Helen slipped through the door. "Come right on in here, Miss Helen. Looks like you can't sleep either."

"I don't see how anyone can sleep with all the flashing and noise going on. You don't think we have a tornado in the vicinity, do you?" She set her lamp on the side table, sat on the settee, and leaned back.

"Don't think so." The elderly housekeeper slipped the needle and thread smoothly through the thick fabric. "Just a spring storm. Nothin' to worry your head about."

Helen gave a little shiver, remembering the close call they'd had the year before. Thanks to their former director, they'd all made it safely to the storm cellar. The only damage had been to the house, and Dr. Trent made sure repairs were made posthaste. "I'm sure you're right. Hope so."

"Got lots on your mind, don't you, honey girl?" Her soft cadence was almost enough to put Helen to sleep right there in her chair.

"No. Just the storm." She lowered her eyes at the half lie.

"Ummm hummm. Just the storm." Virgie rocked and sewed.

"Well, if you must know, I do have thoughts of Mr. Flannigan running through my head." She flashed a look at Virgie, half hoping for advice, half dreading it. When none was forthcoming, she stood. "I'm going to see if there's any lemonade. Would you like a glass?"

"Don't think you goin' to find any. Wasn't any left after supper." She rethreaded her needle and knotted the thread. "Now, I could sure use a cup of tea, though."

"Won't it just heat you up more?"

"Never too hot for tea. It always soothes."

"You're right. That's what I need, too. I'll put the kettle on." Helen picked up her lamp and went to the kitchen.

The large homey room enveloped her with scents of cinnamon and clove. Even the faint smell of lye soap couldn't detract from it.

Helen set the full kettle on the stove and stirred the still-hot coals. It wouldn't take long. She removed a tin of tea leaves from the pantry and put them in a brown porcelain teapot then prepared a tray with cups, saucers, and sugar. Within a few minutes the water was boiling and she poured it over the leaves. By the time she'd strained the tea into the cups and carried the tray to the parlor, her eyelids were getting heavy.

She handed Virgie a cup of the hot brew then sat back on the settee. She sipped and then yawned.

Virgie chuckled. "I think maybe you goin' sleep after all."

Helen smiled. "And I think you knew preparing the tea would make me sleepy."

"I told you tea always soothes. Sometimes before you even get it to your mouth."

"Thank you, Virgie." She took another sip. "I'll just take the cups back to the kitchen then I'm going to go back upstairs."

"No, you're not. You leave that cup right on the tray," Virgie said. "I'll put them away. Go on to sleep now. You got classes to teach in the morning."

Helen rose and stepping over to Virgie, she pressed a kiss on her cheek. "Good night, Virgie. And thank you."

But as sleepy as she was, once she lay on her bed and closed her eyes, dark red curls, sea green eyes, and a tilted smile haunted her thoughts and on into her dreams.

Patrick stared out his bedroom window as rain pelted the hedges around his house. The storm had followed him all the way to Atlanta and showed little sign of stopping anytime soon. If this continued much longer, the rivers could overflow their banks. He only hoped and prayed the deluge had slackened back at Quincy School. Thoughts of the river that flowed across the Quincy property filled him with dread. As far as he knew, the area hadn't flooded in years. But that didn't mean it couldn't happen.

Patrick had seen firsthand how fast river water could rise when he'd traveled to Rome, Georgia, on a business trip a few years earlier. As he'd watched out the window of his third floor hotel room that day, he'd thought he was dreaming as a steamboat floated down Broad Street. Of course Rome was situated between three rivers, but each river had done its own damage.

Perhaps he should have stayed in Mimosa Junction. What would happen there if flooding should occur? Would they be able to evacuate the school in time? He determined to be on the first train to Mimosa Junction in the morning.

After a few hours of fitful sleep, Patrick awoke to sun shining through the window. He breathed a sigh of relief. One day of rain, even a hard rain, shouldn't be enough to bring a river's water levels up.

Patrick began his week finishing up the work on a handmade saddle and shipping off some orders to mail-order customers. Then he turned to checking through his books to calculate how much of his business was mail order. Mail order business shouldn't be affected by a move. *If* he moved. He left instructions with his assistant and told him he'd be back Monday night.

Saturday, he arrived in Mimosa Junction in time for a leisurely lunch in the hotel dining room before his appointment at the hardware store.

An hour later, he walked out the door, a bill of sale and a ring of keys in his hand. And a curious mix of anxiety and excitement in his heart.

Chapter 14

Patrick flinched as rain pelted him from all sides. There hadn't been a cloud in the sky when he'd left town ten minutes ago. He urged his rented horse to a run, shielding his face as well as he could with his hat brim.

By the time he arrived at the school and turned the horse over to Albert, he was drenched from head to toe.

The squishing of his soaked boots as he entered the foyer caused him to cringe. Especially when Virgie walked out of the room to the left with a dusting cloth and stared at him.

With a sheepish, apologetic smile in her direction, he sighed. "I'm sorry about the floor."

A soft chuckle left her lips. "It's all right, Mr. Flannigan. Don't think anythin' about it. Can't be helped in this weather. Wait right there a minute, though."

Dutifully he stood, trying not to move and shake more

water onto the floor, until she returned with a thick braided rug, which she threw down on the floor by his feet.

"You slip off those boots and that hat and throw them on the rug. Then you can go into the infirmary and change into some dry clothes." She motioned to the room she'd just left.

"I have no dry clothes with me, Virgie." Patrick stared down at the water puddling around his feet.

"Don't you worry none. Dr. Trent always keep extras here for when he has to stay over with sick young'uns." She ran an eye over his form. "Just about the same size, I'd say."

A pattering of feet from the stairway drew Patrick's attention and horror filled him as Helen stopped on the first step and gaped at him.

"Looks like you got caught in the downpour." She pressed her lips together but not in time to hide the amused smile on her face.

He must look a sight.

Virgie scowled in her direction. "Don't you worry about it, now. Just run along. I'm goin' to take care of Mr. Flannigan."

"Of course. I'm sorry to have stared." Her eyes danced and she didn't look very sorry. "I'll run up and tell Molly you're here. I don't believe she's expecting you and I know she'll be ecstatic." She spun and hurried up the stairs without another word.

"Don't pay her any mind, Mr. Flannigan." Virgie patted him on the arm. "I don't expect she'd look any better if she got caught in a downpour. Not that you look bad or anythin', of course. Because you don't."

"All right, Virgie. I get the idea. You don't need to worry about my feelings." Patrick slipped out of his boots and tossed his hat on the rug then headed for the infirmary door with the sweet, elderly retainer following behind.

She motioned him to a door in the side wall and he slipped through. She handed him a thick towel then retrieved clothing, including socks and underwear, from a chest in the corner. "Leave them wet clothes on the floor. I'll have one of the maids fetch them and hang them to dry behind the stove in the kitchen. Might take some time. Hope you planned on stayin' awhile." With a smile, she left him alone.

When he was dry and dressed, he ran a comb through his unruly curls, which would be more unruly as soon as they thoroughly dried. No wonder Helen had been amused. He probably looked like a redheaded sheepdog. Still, his heart hammered at the thought of the covert smile. It was quite attractive, even if her humor was directed at him. He headed for the door and went into the foyer again.

Molly ran into his arms with a scream of delight. "Papa! I'm so happy to see you. I didn't know you were coming."

"You didn't?" He pulled back and gave her a look of mock surprise. "I would have thought you'd have heard my heart beating with joy all the way here."

She giggled. "Don't be silly, Papa."

He laughed and glanced around. "Where did Miss Edwards run off to?"

"I think she went to the parlor to sew costumes. I think some of them are for the Easter cantata, you know."

"Oh yes, that's not very far off. I can't wait to see it. And to hear you sing." He tweaked her cheek and she ducked away.

"I only have two lines to sing solo. But I sing them after every verse." She smiled and glanced toward the stairs. "Margaret is to be allowed to sing in the choir, too. But Lily Ann has the lead."

"That's very nice. And I'm happy they are letting Margaret take part." He peered at his daughter. "No more threats?"

She shook her head. "Margaret is very nice, really. We're becoming quite good friends."

"That's good news to hear." He planted a kiss on her forehead." And you're a very good girl, Molly. I'm very pleased with you. And I know Jesus is, too."

She blushed. "Thank you, Papa. Did you wish to speak with Miss Edwards? I can go get her."

"No. I don't want to intrude on her work. It was nothing. I just wanted to greet her."

"I knew it. You like her." She grinned. "You really like her."

He grinned and tugged at one of her braids. "Stop that, little rascal. What would you like to do this afternoon? I'd planned to take you for a ride on the horse, but the rain put a stop to that."

"Hmmm. It's almost dinnertime. After that we have our practice, although Mrs. Quincy probably won't be here unless it stops raining." She put her finger on her cheek and thought. "We could help Sissy and Flora set the table."

"Will they let us?"

"Sure. That's less work for them."

A laugh erupted from his throat. "All right with me. Lead the way."

Silver clinked against china as Sissy and Flora served the chicken soup. Helen thanked Flora and focused on her bowl and spoon. What she'd really been craving lately was chilled cucumber soup. But cucumbers wouldn't be up for a while or any other fresh vegetables, for that matter, although the hot Georgia climate made it possible to have them earlier than the northern states.

Why in the world was she thinking about garden vegetables? She dipped her spoon in the bowl a bit too force-fully, causing a drop to splash onto the tablecloth. Because she didn't want to think about the handsome Patrick Flan-nigan sitting across from her. That was why.

She lifted her head and glanced at him. His curls were still damp from the rain and one of them had curled over his forehead in a perfectly adorable way. She shouldn't have laughed at him. Well, she hadn't really laughed. But she almost had.

Sissy cleared her throat and Helen looked up. Oh dear, she hadn't even noticed when the girl had removed her soup plate. She leaned back slightly so Sissy could serve the main course.

She glanced across the table and met Patrick's eyes. He smiled a lazy smile then turned to his food.

Now why had he smiled like that? As though he had a secret and it involved her. The very idea.

He looked up again and this time she couldn't help re-turn his smile. Her heart sped up. She wondered if she'd have a chance to speak with him today. About Molly's progress, of course. The girl was a delight and always did so well. None of the teachers had complaints about her. Patrick must be very proud of her. It was sad that Molly had no mother to gush over her about her grades. Men seemed to take it for granted their children would do well. She sighed. If she had a child like Molly, she'd be about to burst her buttons with pride.

She pushed away her dessert plate. Well, she didn't have a child of any sort and probably never would.

Patrick was waiting when she stepped into the foyer a few minutes later. She smiled and nodded then started to walk past him.

"Helen." He stepped forward.

"Yes?" she asked, trying to control her breathing.

"Could we talk for a while?" His eyes gazed into hers.

She glanced toward the stairs. "Perhaps the upstairs parlor. It's seldom used except on parents' days."

He offered his arm and she rested her hand there, barely touching.

"Won't Molly be looking for you?"

"I told her I wanted to talk to you then I'd watch the practice." He glanced down at her. "She told me to ask you to come watch as well."

"Of course. I never miss the practices if I can help it." She averted her eyes as they walked up the stairs and turned toward the large sitting room.

When they were seated in matching wing chairs, Patrick turned to her. His eyes seemed to pierce hers, and she felt as though ocean waves would dart out and overcome her at any moment.

"Helen, I can't put this off any longer. I care for you deeply and it's high time you knew it." He took her hand as though afraid she might remove it as she'd done once before. "Is there a chance you might feel some affection for me?"

Her heart pounded hard and happiness washed over her, followed by dread. She lifted up a prayer for wisdom.

"I do care for you. But, Patrick, you live in Atlanta and I don't know if I can leave the school."

He started to speak but stopped and looked at her as though searching her heart. "I know your teaching is very important to you."

She smiled a sad little smile. "As was pointed out to me recently, there are plenty of teachers and the school could do without me quite nicely."

"What? Someone actually said that to you?" His eyes flashed.

"No, no. They didn't mean it as an insult. Just assuring me that if I should decide to leave, the school would go on."

"I see. Then why did you say you couldn't leave the school?"

"It isn't the school, really. It's the children. I love them so much. I don't think I could bear to be away from them."

He blew a breath of air out. "Well, I can't blame you. I'm no match for the children here. I know that."

He dropped her hand and stood. "I appreciate all you are doing for Molly. Perhaps we'll remain friends."

"Wait. Don't you want to hear about Molly's progress this week?"

"Perhaps later. I promised I wouldn't miss her practice." He gave a slight bow and left the room.

But…she hadn't meant the children were more important than he was. Had she? But of course that's practically what she said. Was it true? Were they more important to her than Patrick? She clutched at her throat and swallowed deeply. If not, she'd just given up a chance for happiness with the only man she'd ever loved.

Well, that was that. Patrick was glad Helen hadn't gone to the practice. He wasn't ready to pretend everything was as it had been before. In spite of what he'd said about remaining friends, he wasn't sure if he could do that. His feelings for her were too strong to scale back now.

He'd come close to telling her that he was moving to the Junction. She'd still be near the children. Could even continue to teach some if she wanted to. But he couldn't. Maureen had always been first in his life and he in hers except for God. He couldn't even contemplate entering into a marriage where his wife would put others first.

He sighed and tried to focus on the practice. Mrs. Quincy had made it here after all, driving over with her husband in an enclosed carriage. Molly's voice was true and clear when she sang her solo lines. And Lily Ann sang like an angel, her sightless eyes lifted upward as if she could see into heaven itself and the One to whom she was singing.

The practice ended and Mrs. Quincy stood. "Good job, everyone. I think we're almost ready. Sonny, you were a little late coming in with your verse after Molly's. Try to work on that."

"Yes, ma'am." The ten-year-old boy, who loved to clown, grinned and saluted. Mrs. Quincy shook her head and laughed.

Molly grabbed Patrick's hand and they walked from the auditorium together.

"I wonder why Miss Edwards didn't come to practice. She never misses one." Worry lines puckered the skin between her eyes."

"Something must have come up. You don't need to worry. I was with her an hour ago. She's fine."

Her lips tilted in a half smile. "I'm sure you're right. I'm disappointed she wasn't there. That's all."

The afternoon crawled by for Patrick. He wanted nothing more than to leave before he ran into Helen. He wasn't ready for that. But he didn't want to disappoint Molly and make her sad by leaving right away. Still, he had no intention of being seated across from Helen at supper.

"Papa, guess what we're having for supper?" The lilt in her voice would have told him even if he hadn't already smelled the chicken frying. But he couldn't resist teasing her a little.

"I couldn't guess in a million years. Why don't you tell me?"

She giggled. "Can't you smell that chicken? I've been smelling it for an hour now. It made my tummy growl.

And Sally May said Cook made a caramel pecan cake—my favorite after chocolate."

"That sounds wonderful, sweetie, but since you'll be eating supper an hour sooner than the adults, I believe I might go ahead and leave while the rain has slowed down. I should really take the late train back to Atlanta."

"You mean you won't be here for church in the morning?" Disappointment clouded her beautiful blue eyes.

"Oh, honey. I really need to leave. Does it mean that much to you?"

She nodded. "But it's okay, Papa. I understand if you need to leave tonight."

He groaned inwardly. "Well, maybe I'll wait until tomorrow. After church you and I will eat at the hotel and then I'll take you back to school. I'll take the later afternoon train."

She threw her arms around his neck. "Thank you, Papa. I love going to church with you."

He returned the horse to the livery and asked them to send a horse and carriage around to the hotel in the morning. The rain began again just as he entered the hotel. He glanced up at the sky. Concern ran through him. Maybe the danger of flooding was there after all. He'd see if the rain continued another day. Perhaps he wouldn't be leaving after all.

Chapter 15

By morning, the rain had slowed to a drizzle, but as Patrick stood at the hotel doorway waiting for the carriage, he noticed dark clouds hung low and heavy in the sky. The muddy street in front of the hotel was waterlogged to the point of deep puddles standing everywhere. He was relieved to see no sign that the river had crested, but that didn't mean it wouldn't.

The boy from the livery rode up on a palomino gelding, leading the mare Patrick had used the day before. Patrick pushed the door open and went outside, rain peppering him.

"Morning, Mr. Flannigan. Sorry about the carriage. Mr. Hays said it'd be sure to bog down in the mud."

"It's all right. I'd already thought of that. Planned to exchange the carriage for a horse anyway."

"She's all rested up and ready to go." He handed Patrick the mare's reins then whirled his own mount around and took off down the street.

Patrick stood in the muddy street trying to decide if he should ride to the school or go ahead and board the train for Atlanta. But no, he couldn't chance it. If the river overflowed its banks, the school would be at risk.

He mounted up and headed down the street. This time, he wore a rain slicker in case the drizzle turned into a downpour again.

As he passed his new place of business, he grinned. Molly would be tickled, but he wouldn't tell her yet. He didn't want it to get back to Helen that he was moving. If she decided to change her mind, he wanted it to be because she loved him. After all that was the main reason he'd bought the store and made plans to move his business. He loved her and wanted to spend his life with her in a place she'd be happy.

The thought ran through him that perhaps he should make it easier for her and tell her the truth. But stubbornness bit at him and he shoved the thought away.

Helen glanced toward the classroom window and breathed a breath of relief. It appeared they were in for a long, slow rain today rather than more storms as she'd feared. She lifted her hand to her lips and patted back a yawn. Between the storm outside and the storm within her own heart, she'd slept very little last night.

Had she done the right thing by refusing to form a relationship beyond friendship with Patrick? It seemed the only practical thing to do, at least at the time, but through the night her heart and thoughts had lashed at her. She'd given up her chance at love and marriage to the only man who'd touched her heart and soul.

But what else could she have done? Of course, another

teacher could meet the children's educational needs. But emotionally she was tied to them and they to her, weren't they? She'd been with them for several years now. One by one their faces had drifted before her closed eyelids. Of course the three she was most concerned about were Molly, Lily Ann, and Margaret. She felt that she could help Margaret through whatever emotional trauma she was suffering.

She started as a snore sounded from the rear of the room. Jeremiah was sound asleep, his head lolling to the side. She shook her head and headed back to his desk. She touched his shoulder and he jerked, his eyes big and darting from side to side.

He looked up and relief crossed his face. "Sorry, Miz Edwards," he said, in broken English. She nodded and smiled. "It's all right, Jeremiah. Didn't you sleep well last night?"

He shook his head.

"Neither did I." She gave him a pat. "But we'll both have to do the best we can to stay awake. Why don't you go get a drink of water and see if that helps?"

He nodded and went to the stand in the corner. She cringed as he slurped from the glass.

Helen gathered up the English papers and returned to her desk. It would be dinnertime in a few minutes. She was glad she only had one class this afternoon. Perhaps she could find time for a nap. Probably not, though. Virgie needed help finishing the costumes. Easter was only a couple of weeks away.

Most of the children wouldn't be going home for the holiday since it was a short one, but many of the parents came to spend the day here with their children. The Easter program was always a big event for the school—even more so since Abigail had taken over the music and drama department.

When the class was finally over, she dismissed the children and went to her room to freshen up for the midday meal.

She washed her face at the basin and blotted it with a soft towel. Her eyes strayed longingly to her soft bed. She sighed and headed for the door.

When she entered the dining room she stopped short at the sight of Patrick seated between Molly and Howard. She hastened to her chair, her heart hammering wildly. Why hadn't he left for Atlanta?

During the meal, she tried to listen to Patrick's conversation with Howard, but Felicity and Hannah, who were seated near her, kept up a constant chatter about the weather and the upcoming holiday.

"I hope the rain lets up before Easter." Hannah took a sip of her tomato soup. "It would be a shame if some of the parents couldn't come."

"Oh, I'm sure it won't last that long." Felicity reached over and patted the young woman's hand. "Spring rains come and go this time of year. And storms can burst out at any moment. But they seldom last long."

Helen wasn't so sure. If the rains didn't slow down soon, the river could overflow its banks. And the school was in a valley. Flooding wasn't probable, but it was possible.

The children filed out of the dining room, following Charles and Hannah. Helen stepped to the door at the same moment as Patrick. He stood back and let her pass through the door. With misery nearly overwhelming her, she ducked her head and stepped into the foyer.

"Helen?"

At the sound of Patrick's voice, she turned. "Yes?"

"I know you need to get to your class and I'll be leaving

for Atlanta later this afternoon, but I wanted to ask you to at least think about what we discussed."

The consternation in his eyes matched that in her heart, but a glimmer of hope rose inside her. Was there still a chance? Was there a way to work this out?

"Yes, Patrick. I will."

He reached for her hand and pressed his lips to her palm. "Thank you."

Her heart thumped wildly as she went upstairs. *Oh, God, show me what to do. I love him so much. If there is a way for us, please show me.*

By midafternoon, the sun came out brightly and the temperature was a little cooler than before the rain. That was good. A month or so from now, rain would only make things hot and humid.

Helen stepped out onto the porch for a breath of fresh air, but the chairs were all damp so she went inside and gravitated to the parlor.

Virgie was half asleep in her rocking chair, her hands resting on the pile of fabric on her lap. She started awake as Helen sat across from her.

Virgie yawned and shook her head from side to side. "This weather making me sleepy as a bear in winter. Pourin' down rain one minute, sun streamin' down the next. Wish it would make up its mind."

"I hope the rain is over for a while."

"I do, too. Seems like everything in the house is damp. It isn't, but it sure do feel like it."

Helen retrieved the vest she'd worked on the day before from the basket by her chair. "I know. If it isn't rain in the spring, it's humidity in the summer."

Virgie chuckled the soft deep laugh Helen loved to hear. "Listen to us, complaining and jawin' about the weather like that's goin' to change anything."

Nodding, Helen sewed a button on the vest. "Do you have any idea of what Abigail has in mind for these costumes? They don't look much like Easter costumes to me. You'd think she'd want white and gold for the angels."

"The Easter costumes are already done." Virgie lifted an eyebrow. "These are for the end of school program."

Helen paused. "Maybe I just assumed they were for Easter because the Easter cantata is coming up. Perhaps she plans to do the end-of-school play we'd discussed about the Quincy family.

"Well, I s'pose we'll just have to wait and see." Virgie cast a glance at Helen. "You seem all out of sorts. What wrong with you?"

"Oh, I'm all right. Just struggling with some difficult decisions." Helen avoided Virgie's piercing glance and focused on sewing another button tightly in place.

"Would it be somethin' about a redheaded Irishman?"

"Maybe." Helen put down the vest and stood. "Oh, I'm not in the mood for sewing. I think I'll go for a walk."

"Mighty soggy out there. You likely to sink right down into the mud." Virgie pursed her lips and squinted her eyes as she threaded her needle again.

"Well then, maybe I'll go to my room and read for a while. I'll help sew tomorrow. If Abigail doesn't intend them for Easter, there's probably no hurry."

Instead of heading upstairs, she went outside. Virgie was right. The yard and lane looked like a bog. But at least the porch furniture was dry now. She settled onto one of the white wicker rockers and soon the rhythmic cadence of motion began to soothe her anxious thoughts.

The door opened and Margaret came out with Hannah. They were so intent in their conversation they didn't notice her.

"Hmmm. I don't think we can go for a walk, Margaret." Hannah's cheerful voice carried across the porch. "It's much too muddy."

"Then let's sit out here on the porch." They turned. "Oh, Miss Edwards." Disappointment was obvious in Margaret's voice as she stared at Helen.

Helen rose. "If you two need a quiet spot to visit, this is the very place. I was just going in."

"Thanks, Helen," Hannah said. "But you're welcome to join us if you like." The halfhearted tone belied her words.

Helen smiled. "Another time, perhaps. I have some letters I wish to write before supper."

She trudged upstairs to her room. It seemed as though Hannah was getting along quite well with Margaret. She hadn't seen the girl with such a big smile in a long time. Perhaps P.J. was right. Maybe a younger woman like Hannah was just what Margaret needed.

As she reached the second floor landing, Molly and Patrick were coming down from the third floor.

"Miss Edwards, I've been showing Papa my new drawing." Molly's face glowed with pleasure. "And he loved it. Didn't you, Papa?"

"I sure did, sugar. It's one of the prettiest live oak trees I've ever seen."

Helen smiled. "Molly drew it from memory. I'm sure you recognized it."

"Of course. It was the tree by the gate." The look he gave her was tender. "I know I'll miss sitting in its shade."

Helen blushed at the memory of her hand snug and warm in his before she'd pulled it away. Yes, she'd miss the tree, too.

"P.J. is going to let us plant another one in the same spot."

"That's a good idea." His lips curved into a smile that

also flashed in his eyes. "I wonder how long it takes a live oak tree to grow to the size of that one."

"At least twenty-five years, Papa," Molly said. "We looked it up in our science book."

He nodded. "That's much too long. We need to move the bench."

Helen burst out laughing. "We definitely need to move the bench."

"What's so funny about that?" Molly looked from Helen to Patrick, a confused look on her face. "Anyway, we've already moved the bench. It's under the magnolia tree on the other side of the gate."

"Oh yes, I think I did see the faithful bench when I rode up the lane this morning." He cut a glance at Helen. "Too bad it's so muddy down that way. We could try it out."

Helen bit her lip to keep from smiling. "Pay no attention to your father, Molly. I think he's being a little silly today."

Patrick's laughter rang out. She loved it when he seemed happy like he did today.

"I suppose you'll be leaving now that the rain has stopped. As you can see, we're perfectly all right."

"Yes, I hate to leave, but I do have a business to run." He turned his gaze fully on Helen. "I would like to talk to you about something before I go."

"Flannigan."

Patrick turned to look toward the caller.

"There you are." Dr. Trent came up the stairs, a serious look on his face. "I was wondering if you could do me a favor. It's rather an emergency."

"Of course. Glad to help any way I can."

"I need to check on one of the Blaine boys on the other side of Campville, but I also need to get some medicine to an elderly lady in Mimosa Junction." He shook his head. "Of course, these things happen sometimes, but since you're going there anyway, I was hoping perhaps you could drop the medicine off for me so I won't be so late getting home to Abigail."

Patrick darted a quick glance at Helen and a flash of disappointment shadowed his eyes, but he smiled as he replied. "Yes, of course I will, Dr. Trent."

Relief washed over Dr. Trent's face. "If you'll come to the infirmary with me, I'll get the bottle of medicine for you. I can't tell you how much I appreciate this."

"Please, don't give it another thought. I'm glad to help." He sent a smile of regret to Helen then opened his arms to his daughter, who flew into his embrace. "I'll try to come next weekend. But if not, then at least the one after that."

With a final kiss on Molly's cheek, Patrick headed down the stairs.

Helen put her arm around Molly and they stood together and watched him until he entered the infirmary.

At a sniffle from Molly, Helen drew her closer. "It's all right, sweetie. We'll find some way to make the time go by in a hurry. He'll be back before we know it."

But what had he wanted to talk to her about? Had he changed his mind about waiting for an answer? If he had, would she have been able to make a decision?

She patted Molly's shoulder. "At least it's not raining."

Chapter 16

It was the final practice. Easter was tomorrow and the cantata would be held after dinner. Helen sat in the back of the auditorium. Abigail turned and gave her a questioning look. Helen held her clasped hands up in victory. The neighbors had all been invited, in addition to the families and the staff, so the room would be full. Abigail had been a little nervous about the children's voices carrying all the way to the rear of the room, but Helen could hear them just fine.

She kept darting glances toward the door behind her. Patrick hadn't come last weekend after all. He'd promised to be here this weekend, but Saturday was half over. Molly would be devastated if he wasn't here for the program. And to be honest, so would she. After searching her heart, she'd decided if he still wanted to court her, she would agree. Who knew? Maybe if they spent a lot of time together, they'd decide they didn't care as much for each other as they thought.

A short laugh escaped her lips. No chance of that on her part. She'd missed him so much these couple of weeks she'd had trouble keeping her thoughts on her teaching.

After watching Margaret develop an attachment to Hannah that bordered on hero worship and with Abigail spending more time with Lily Ann again, Helen realized the school would do fine without her if her relationship with Patrick developed that far. P.J. would make sure everything was always in tip-top shape, and Dr. Trent was always here whenever he was needed.

She would miss all the children and staff terribly, but she doubted they'd miss her much after the first few weeks. Life would go on for all of them. And perhaps she'd finally have a husband and child to love. For Molly was already like a daughter to her. And she was still young enough to have more children.

The doors creaked open and Patrick sat down beside her. Heat rushed to her face. Oh dear, she already had them married with children and he wasn't even courting her yet.

"Sorry to be so late," he whispered. "I had some things to tie up before I left Atlanta."

"You're just in time. The song they're getting ready to sing is the one with Molly's solos."

The choir started the song beautifully; then Molly stepped forward. Her glance surveyed the room, finally reaching the back. When she recognized her father, her eyes lit up for a moment then she began to sing the verse. Patrick applauded as she stepped back and the choir joined in the rest of the song.

Lily Ann was at home with a sore throat and instructions from Dr. Trent to gargle often and eat spoonsful of honey and lemon. Abigail and Helen were praying she wouldn't have to miss the cantata. But the child's health had to come first.

When practice was over and the children dismissed, Molly made a beeline for Patrick and threw her arms around him. "Papa, I was afraid you weren't coming."

He put his arm around her as they left the auditorium. "I said I'd be here, didn't I, princess?"

"Yes, but sometimes things happen beyond our control."

Patrick looked at his daughter with amazement then glanced at Helen. "I think my daughter is growing up."

"Yes, that happens." Helen laughed. "She's certainly wise for one so young."

Molly made a sound of exasperation. "You two don't have to talk about me as though I'm not here."

Patrick's eyes danced. "I beg your pardon, young lady, and to make up for my lack of manners, how would you like to go to the hotel for ice cream? I happen to know they have some today."

"Yes, I'd love some ice cream." Molly clapped her hands in very childlike fashion.

"And I'm sure you'd like for Miss Edwards to join us?" He flashed a grin in Helen's direction.

Before Helen could accept, Abigail joined them. "Helen, would you mind helping me this afternoon? I have some finishing touches on the sets to make and Trent was called away earlier."

Disappointment seared Helen to the point that she almost made an excuse to say no. But then shame washed over her. Abigail had worked so hard to make the program wonderful for them all. Even in her condition, she'd kept going. Helen couldn't be selfish.

"Yes, of course, I will." She smiled at Patrick and Molly. "Can we make it another time?"

Patrick grinned. "Yes, we can. Could we talk later?"

Helen nodded. "After supper?"

"It's a date." He turned to Molly and offered his arm. "I guess it's you and me, milady."

Abigail's face was a picture of consternation as they walked away. "Oh, Helen, I'm so sorry. You should have told me you had plans. Go on with them. I'll find someone else to help."

For a moment, Helen was tempted, but it would be a good thing for Molly and Patrick to spend some time alone. And the staff was busy. There might be no one to help Abigail.

"Nonsense, I didn't have plans, really. Patrick was just being kind." She looped her arm through her friend's and walked with her back to the auditorium.

"How many parents are coming early?" Abigail stopped halfway to the stage, panting. "Are you all right?" Concern ripped through Helen as she eyed her friend's moist forehead.

"Yes," Abigail gave a half-gasp, half-laugh. "I get winded a lot easier these days."

Helen ran her gaze down Abigail's still trim figure. "Are you wearing a corset?"

"Of course. I can't let the children see my big stomach."

"Abigail, that's not good for you. Does Dr. Trent know you're wearing that tight thing?"

"Actually this is the first time I've worn it and he left before I put it on." She bit her lip. "Mrs. Carey says every woman must wear them."

"Well, Mrs. Carey is a million years old and probably doesn't know what she's talking about."

Abigail frowned. "She used to be the midwife before there was a doctor around here. Some women still use her to deliver their babies."

"Some women don't know any better. But you do, and

you know very well you shouldn't be wearing a corset when you're with child." Helen heaved a sigh. "That's medieval. Or old fashioned, anyway. Why don't you go in the back parlor and slip out of it. You can put it back on to go home."

"Oh, all right."

When they reached the stairs, Abigail went to the parlor and changed.

She laughed as she rejoined Helen in the auditorium. "You were right, of course. I feel much better."

Relief coursed through Helen. "I should think so. Now I'll answer your question. We're expecting five sets of parents here tonight. Virgie has the maids preparing rooms for them. The others will arrive in the morning, some before church and some afterward."

"Hmmm. If the school keeps growing, there won't be room for them to stay the night here in the future."

"Maybe. There are seven empty rooms on the second floor and we still have half-a-dozen unused ones on this floor. Although they aren't fixed up yet." Helen glanced around. "What do you need me to do now?"

"Did you have fun, pumpkin?" Patrick patted Molly's hand where it rested on the carriage seat beside him.

"Yes, but it would have been nice if Miss Edwards could have come with us." Molly turned her hand over and clutched Patrick's.

"I know, sweetie. But there will be other times." At least, Patrick hoped so. The day had been full of frustrations. He'd hoped by now to have let her know about his purchase of the hardware store and his plans to relocate to Mimosa Junction. But every time he'd thought he would have a chance to talk to her, they were interrupted, just as they'd been the last time he was here. He sighed. Maybe tonight.

A sudden clap of thunder interrupted his thoughts and caused Molly to jump. She sat up straight and clutched his hand tighter as the thunder continued to rumble and roll. Lightning flashed in the distance.

Patrick snapped the reins and the horses broke into a run. Even with the top up he didn't want to get caught in a thunderstorm with Molly in the carriage.

The first drops fell as they pulled up in front of the school. He walked inside with Molly then drove the carriage to the barn.

Albert cast a worried glance up to the sky as he took the reins. "You may as well plan to stay the night, Mr. Flannigan. Road's already muddy. Can't take much more rain without flooding into the fields and bogging down all the carriage wheels. I plan to bed down in the back room here myself."

"I'll see how it goes, Albert. I might just ride one of the horses to town if it doesn't get too bad." The words were barely out of his mouth when the sky opened up. With a wave at Albert, he took off running to the house. He pushed through the door and stood dripping on the floor. *Not again.*

Sally May came ambling into the foyer, her eyes big. "Whoo-wee. You better stand there while I get some towels. And get them shoes off, Mr. Flannigan, before Virgie sees that puddle on her floor."

Patrick chuckled but did her bidding. A few minutes later he repeated the same actions as the last time, only with Sally May as his guide instead of Virgie.

When he stepped back into the foyer wearing Dr. Trent's clothing once again, Virgie stood there with a twinkle in her eyes.

"I see Sally May took good care of you." She gave a nod of approval.

"Yes, she did. But I think her main motive was to keep you from being upset over the floor." He grinned. "You must be a mean woman around here, Miz Virgie."

Virgie gave one of her soft velvety laughs. "I might be or maybe they just want me to be happy."

"I think the latter the most likely reason." He glanced toward the stairs as a middle-aged couple came down with one of the boys between them. His eyes were shining as he walked between them.

"Some of the parents are already here, I see," he said.

"All of them that's coming tonight. It's nice to see the children with their mamas and papas." Virgie smiled at the couple. "The dining room right through that door. You sit anywhere you like and Bobby can sit with you."

At the sound of footsteps on the stairs, Patrick glanced up again, eagerly hoping to see Helen.

"She be down in a minute." Virgie's look of amusement sent a heat wave to his face.

"Who?"

She chuckled. "Who, indeed? I might have meant Miss Molly, mightn't I?"

"You might have, but you didn't, did you?"

"Ain't no sense in being embarrassed about it. She a sweet lady and mighty pretty, too. And you a handsome, strappin' fellow." She looked him up and down. "Nothin' wrong with it at all. You marry that gal."

Laughter rose in Patrick's heart. She'd hit the nail on the head. "Trouble is I'm not sure she'll have me, Virgie."

Virgie gave a little snort. "She'll have you. Be crazy if she don't. And there she come now." She walked away toward the kitchen, humming.

Helen's face radiated a very attractive pink blush and

her eyes shone a welcome. He could only hope he wasn't misreading her.

"Molly will be right down. And she said don't wait for her." Her upturned face glowed.

"In that case, shall we go on in? I'm suddenly very hungry. The ice cream didn't stay with me long." He held out his arm and tucked her small, soft hand in the crook of it. Somehow it felt like it belonged there.

He held her chair and then claimed the chair next to her. He didn't care who usually sat there.

She blushed and ducked her head but failed to hide the pretty smile that tilted her lips. "Poor Felicity. You've taken her chair."

"I'm sure she'll find another with no problem." He squeezed her hand and then released it before anyone could see. "I decided, with all the guests here tonight, I'd take my opportunity to sit where I like. Besides, I heard Virgie tell some parents to sit anywhere."

"Well, if Virgie said it, then it must be all right. She sets the rules in the household."

Molly appeared at his elbow. "Papa, will you please scoot over and let me sit between you and Miss Edwards?"

Patrick held back a sigh and heard Helen cough in an obvious attempt not to laugh. He moved over a seat and Molly scooted in.

"Thank you." She turned to Helen, excitement in her voice. "Isn't it fun having all the parents here?"

Helen nodded. "Yes, it certainly is. I'm so glad we opened up the third floor and made all the changes. Otherwise we wouldn't have had room."

Sissy and two other servers came in and served the soup.

Patrick listened to the murmur of voices around the

table and wished the meal was over so he could be alone with Helen and tell her his news.

However, once more his plans were upset. After supper, it was pouring down rain outside and there were too many people inside to find a private place. Finally he settled down beside her in the front parlor and simply enjoyed being near her as they visited with Hannah and Charles. Virgie was too busy to join them, and Patrick rather missed the soft cadence of her voice and her gentle humor.

He told Helen good night on the second floor landing then went up to the small room he'd been assigned at the end of the other wing.

He was happy to see a Bible on the nightstand as his was back at the hotel. He sat on a comfortable chair by the window and opened the small book. He found his way to the seventh chapter of Luke, where he'd left off the night before. He laid the Bible down and crawled between crisp sheets.

Lord, if You want me to marry this woman I love so much, please work it out. If not, please give me the peace to accept Your will.

He'd found her eyes resting on him more than once today. Hope rose in his heart. He was almost sure she felt the same way he did. And he knew he loved her very much.

Peace washed over him in spite of the rain that pelted the roof and hit against the windows.

One thing he knew. Tomorrow he'd do everything in his power to find a way to talk to her in private.

Chapter 17

The sound of rain beating against the window woke Helen from a sound sleep. Would it ever stop? And on Easter Sunday.

She jumped out of bed and ran to the window. She could barely make out the shape of the barn through the pounding rain. A clap of thunder rent the air, followed by a flash of lightning that seemed to light up the backyard and the woods beyond. Trees swayed and bent from the force of the wind. She backed away from the window.

She lit a lamp in the darkened room and picked up the watch from her side table. Six o'clock already. Quickly she washed her face and hands then dressed in one of her Sunday dresses. They wouldn't likely be going to church in the storm, but she still wanted to look her best.

She stood in front of the wood-framed mirror on a stand in the corner. She pulled and twisted her hair this way and that. Finally, she wound it into a loose chignon on the back of her neck and allowed tendrils of curls to hang down the sides of her face.

She gave herself a critical look and shrugged. She didn't have time to stand here primping. There were guests in the house. Perhaps they could hold some sort of service in the auditorium after breakfast.

She found a scattering of people in the dining room, including Charles and Patrick. Patrick stood at the buffet, filling a cup with hot coffee from the large silver urn.

He turned around and their eyes met. He smiled. She blushed and returned his smile then sat on the chair he held out for her. Right beside his.

"Good morning, Helen." Charles tossed her a bright smile. She never had understood how he could be so friendly after she'd turned him down. Perhaps he realized he wasn't that interested in having a relationship with her after all.

Sonny's parents came through the door, followed by all the others. Perhaps none of them had been sure about venturing in alone. After all, this was a first overnight stay for all of them.

"I wonder if the other parents will be able to get here?" The question had been buzzing around her mind since she'd seen the weather.

"I wouldn't count on that." Patrick shook his head. "I rode down the lane when I woke up to check it out. It appears the road is washed out in several places. And the low spots are flooded. I don't think anyone is coming in or going out."

Felicity, who had just entered and sat at the table, gasped. "Are you sure?"

"I'm afraid so."

"Oh no." Helen's brow furrowed. "The children will be so disappointed."

"Well, perhaps the big meal and the program will cheer them up a little," Howard said, "although I know that won't take the place of their parents being here."

Charles returned to the table after getting more coffee. "I don't think many more were coming, anyway. A couple, maybe. The others live too far away to make the trip more than to pick up their children at Christmas and for summer break."

Helen clapped her hands to her face. "Oh no. This means Dr. Trent and Abigail can't come either. How will we have the cantata without Abigail?"

Felicity grinned. "Guess it's up to you. You've been with Abigail nearly every practice."

"But…I can't."

"Of course, you can." P.J. stood in the doorway and had obviously heard every word. "I have every confidence in you."

"What about Lily Ann's solo?" Helen knew she was working herself into a panic. "They won't be able to come, either."

"You'll just have to get someone else to sing her solo." P.J. found a seat next to Sonny and his parents.

Sissy and two other servers brought covered dishes and set them on the buffet. The aroma of scrambled eggs, sausage, and ham made Helen realize how hungry she was. She waited and let the guests go first.

As soon as her filled plate was before her, she focused her attention on the delicious food while she pondered her problem. There was only one student who could do as well as Lily Ann on the solo—Margaret.

Helen glanced across the table at the director and then switched her vision to Margaret, who sat beside her parents. She wondered if P.J. had spoken to them, yet. It would make the situation easier for her if Margaret could fill Lily Ann's spot.

After breakfast some of the men, including Patrick, went to check the water level at the river. Helen breathed a sigh of relief. She knew Patrick wanted to talk to her, and she was eager to let him know she'd decided to agree to the courtship. But today wasn't shaping up to be a good day for that.

She hurried down the hall to the director's office and tapped on the door.

When she was seated across from P.J., she took a deep breath.

P.J. smiled. "You want to know if Margaret can be in the cantata."

"Well, I don't want to go against any decision you might have made, of course, but it would be nice if we had her lovely voice in there, since Lily Ann won't be here." She cast an eager look in the director's direction.

"As a matter of fact, I've had a quite satisfactory meeting with Margaret and her parents. I'm convinced nothing like the former episode will happen again. I also believe Margaret is truly sorry and she's suffered enough." She smiled. "So if you'd like to ask her to be a stand-in if Lily Ann can't make it, you have my permission."

"Wonderful!" Helen jumped up. "I'll ask her now. She's probably with her parents somewhere."

"I believe they were going to look at the science exhibit from last fall. Charles has displayed it again for the parents that didn't get a chance to see it."

"Thank you, P.J. You're a wonderful woman and we're lucky to have you as our director."

"Oh, go along with you." She waved her hand toward the door. "I'm a mean tyrant and everyone knows it."

Helen laughed as she sailed out the door and went in search of Margaret and her parents.

The rain had finally slowed down to a slight drizzle. As Patrick stood near the bank of the river with Charles and Howard, he heaved a breath of relief. The river hadn't crested, so if the rain stopped, they wouldn't need to worry about any major flooding. But the rain itself had been a real gully-washer and the road was almost impassible in spots. As soon as the rain stopped and the sun came out they could start filling the holes in the lane with gravel. Until then the house guests would have to be patient and stay put.

They returned to the house. Patrick still held out some hope of talking to Helen. But if she had to be in charge of the Easter program, he wasn't sure if an opportunity would arise. Besides, with the house full of extra people it would be difficult to find a private place to talk. He went in search of Molly and found her and Trudy in their room in an animated conversation.

Both girls jumped up when they saw him.

"Mr. Flannigan, guess?" Trudy turned big brown eyes on him.

"Hmmm. You just found out you're really a long-lost princess from some never before heard of kingdom."

Trudy giggled. "No. Guess again."

"Oh, Papa." Molly gave him a look of disdain which quickly changed into a smile and a giggle. "Margaret has been given her freedom."

"Yes. I know. Because her parents are here."

"No, not that. She's all the way free, now. Even when her parents leave. But that's not all."

"Oh, there's more? I think that's pretty big news as it is." And he wasn't too sure how he felt about it. After all, the girl had terrorized his daughter. A twinge of guilt bit at him. He'd forgiven her for that.

"It is," Trudy said, "but there's more. Margaret gets to be in the cantata and she'll sing the solo if Lily Ann can't come because of the weather."

"Or because she may still be sick," Molly added.

"Okay, that's very nice for Margaret. Not too great for poor Lily Ann."

"But, Papa. Lily Ann would want what's best for the cantata. And everyone knows Margaret has the best voice after Lily Ann."

"So how do you girls feel about Margaret not being punished anymore?" He thought he could tell what the answer would be. Molly and Trudy had apparently forgiven and forgotten and were quite ready to be friends with the girl again.

"We're happy, Papa." Molly smiled broadly. "Margaret is sorry for what she did and we're all best friends again."

Trudy nodded. "We missed her," she frowned, "but she'd better not ever threaten to hurt Lily Ann again. And we told her so."

Patrick blinked back sudden tears and coughed loudly. "I'm proud of you girls."

"Miss Shepherd says we should always forgive when someone trespasses against us." Trudy's face was suddenly solemn. "Because we all need forgiveness."

"Miss Shepherd sounds like a very wise woman. Just who is she, by the way?"

"Our Sunday school teacher, Papa. Remember, you met her a few weeks ago."

"Oh yes, the preacher's daughter. And I'm glad you took her words to heart." He reached over and gave one of Molly's braids a yank.

Molly nodded. "I wish we could have gone to church

today. It doesn't seem right to miss. Especially on Easter Sunday."

"Well, next Sunday will be here before you know it."

Patrick left and ambled over to his room where he removed his wet shoes and dried them the best he could. He hung his socks in front of the stove and stretched out on the bed. He hoped the weather would be nice this week. He planned to get the shop ready this week and start bringing supplies over from the Atlanta store. He hoped to have everything moved and the other store cleared out within two or three weeks. Most everything would come by rail.

He drifted off to sleep with thoughts of Helen and the possible look on her face when he told her the news.

Margaret's voice drifted across the auditorium with angelic tones. Helen couldn't keep the smile from her face. What a gift the child had received from God. The audience seemed mesmerized. When the solo was over and the choir joined in for the final song, Helen dabbed at her eyes with a lacy handkerchief.

She and the boys in the group stayed after everyone else had left the room to fold chairs and put them away. She didn't really need to stay, but it gave her a chance to reflect. The cantata had definitely been a success. Now that it was over, and she knew she'd given it her all, she could refocus her thoughts where they truly wanted to go.

Patrick. Would they finally get a chance to talk so she could tell him? She sighed. The possibility didn't look too promising. The house was still full of people. Perhaps tomorrow.

After a delicious supper which proved to be nearly as sumptuous as their Easter dinner had been, most of the guests retired to their rooms. A few, however, joined the teaching staff in the large parlor for music where Hannah played the piano and the others joined in singing hymns. The evening flew by, and all too soon it was time to say good night.

Classes wouldn't resume until Tuesday, so the children had been allowed to stay up longer than usual in honor of their parents' visit.

Helen could only hope the roads would be passable by Tuesday. She couldn't imagine trying to hold classes if the guests were still here. The children would never be able to concentrate knowing their parents were downstairs.

As she stepped into the foyer, she found Patrick waiting. Everyone else had already disappeared up the stairs.

"Helen. I thought we'd never have a chance to say hello without dozens of people around." He took her hand tentatively as though he wasn't sure if he'd be allowed to keep it in his.

Helen smiled and let her hand remain in his. She could feel the calluses on his palm and was surprised to find the sensation rather pleasant. "I've been wanting to talk to you, too, Patrick, but I only have a moment. It's very late."

"I know. Besides, it wouldn't do to have anyone misunderstand. So for now, let me merely say, I have a great deal of admiration for you and hope we can let our friendship grow into something more. I have some news for you, but it will keep until a more opportune time."

"I have something important to say to you as well. But I don't want to wait. Let me just say that my answer to your earlier question is yes. I'd be honored to consider our friendship to be a courtship."

Light filled his eyes and the grin on his face spoke volumes. He opened his mouth to say something, but she pressed two fingers against his lips.

"Good night, Patrick. We'll talk tomorrow." She turned and ran up the stairs and into her room.

Oh dear. Had she been too bold? She stood against the closed door, her breath coming in excited little pants. What if he'd changed his mind? But he certainly didn't look like he had, with that big old Cheshire cat grin on his face.

A little giggle escaped through her lips. It seemed everytime she was near him she giggled about something. She hadn't done that for years.

Suddenly she noticed how stuffy the room was. She'd closed the window earlier to keep out the rain, but now she flung it open wide and breathed deeply of the clean, fresh air. A cow mooed from nearby. Albert had probably opened the barn door for the same reason she'd flung the window wide. Nothing smelled like rain-washed air. Maybe the storms were over. Probably not, though. It was still early April. She wondered what Atlanta was like this time of year. Could she be happy living there? Being so used to country sounds and sights and smells? A vision of tight, dark red curls and sea green eyes drifted through her thoughts. And a smile that curled her toes. Oh yes, she could be happy in Timbuktu or the jungles of Africa, as long as Patrick Flannigan was by her side. She smiled. *And a sweet daughter like Molly.* She would take good care of her adopted daughter and teach her everything she would need to make her life as easy as possible. A home in Atlanta would be just fine.

She undressed in the moonlight and changed into her nightgown. She crawled into bed between crisp, cool sheets and sank her head into her soft feather pillow.

Chapter 18

Patrick whistled an old Irish tune as he shoveled sand into holes in the lane leading to the school. He hoped the gravel could be filled in before the next rain or the sand would all be washed away. But it was at least a temporary solution and would allow the parents to return home. All he'd thought about most of the night and all morning was his anticipated meeting with Helen. Her morning classes would be over soon and he only hoped she was free this afternoon, because he absolutely had to get the new building ready and get back to Atlanta to finish up there.

He finished filling two more holes then headed for the house. He was glad that so many men in the neighborhood had volunteered to help.

He washed up in the infirmary and changed into his own clothing, which Sissy had handed him as he'd walked in.

He entered the dining room and found Helen already

seated. Her eyes lit up when she saw him. He took the chair next to hers. "Can we talk after dinner?"

"Yes, I'm free all afternoon." Her voice had a little lilt and his heart sped up. Even though she didn't know she wouldn't have to leave the area, she was willing to go with him. He was glad she wouldn't have to make that sacrifice.

Good. Now if they could find a private place to talk. He glanced around. One of the couples had already left for their home. He was pretty sure the rest would leave after the meal, now that the lane was passable.

For the first time in days, he actually enjoyed food. Amazing, the difference a few words from Helen had made. The gumbo was delicious and a fresh garden salad tingled on his palate. Fried ham and buttered sweet potatoes followed, with green beans that he would call fried. However they were prepared, they were delicious. The ever-present sweet tea refreshed him after the hard work of the morning. And Selma's peach cobbler with sweet cream whipped into soft peaks topped off the meal.

After the meal, he said his farewells to Molly, promising a surprise the following week, which curbed her tears.

A half hour later, the children had all returned to their classrooms and the parents had made their exits, among a lot of relieved laughter. Most said they had a wonderful time in spite of it all, but they hoped their return trip in May would be uneventful.

Patrick stood on the porch with Helen. "Shall we sit here or walk down the lane to the bench?"

"Oh. Let's walk down. I haven't had a chance to rest there since the other tree was removed."

"Fine with me. Let's see if the magnolia has as much shade as the live oak did."

The magnolia proved to have a great deal more shade than the live oak. One could have almost hidden on the bench beneath the blossom-laden branches. This was fine with Patrick because two men were working on the lane just a short distance farther along.

He waited while Helen smoothed her skirt then seated himself beside her on the bench. "It's been a disturbing couple of days, hasn't it?" Oh, that was brilliant. After waiting so long for this opportunity, he wasted it making small talk.

"Yes, it's been dreadful." She fanned her hand in front of her face and tapped her fingers on the wooden bench. "I certainly hope the storms are over."

"So do I." He reached over and took her hand. "Helen, there's something I need to tell you."

Her face paled and she inhaled sharply. "It's quite all right, Patrick. I understand if you've changed your mind about wanting to go beyond friendship." Misery and embarrassment were written all over her face.

"What?" Shocked, he lifted her chin and looked into her eyes. "Not at all. Why would you think that?"

"Well, I was afraid you'd think I was being too bold by saying what I said to you last night."

"No, of course not. You were enchanting. I've thought of nothing else since."

"Really?" A faint blush tinged her cheek.

Didn't she have any idea how he felt about her? He sighed. How could she? They'd talked very little about anything other than the school and how Molly was getting along. "Helen, I didn't intend to be so abrupt. I wanted to give you a proper courtship, but the truth of the matter is I'm in love with you and it's time you knew it. I want to marry you, if you'll have me."

She smiled. A joyful smile that sent his heart racing. "I love you, too, Patrick. And I want you to know that I will gladly go with you to Atlanta or anywhere else you wish to go. I don't care where I live, so long as I'm with you and Molly."

He pressed her hand to his lips. "Well, you won't have to. Because that's what I wanted to tell you. I'm moving to Mimosa Junction. I've already purchased a building for my shop and plan to start moving things here this week."

Wonder crossed her face. "You would do that for me? But Patrick, you don't have to. I know your business is already established in Atlanta."

"And it will be just as established in Mimosa Junction. To be honest, when I first started thinking about the idea, it was mainly because of you. But the more time I've spent in this area, the more I like it." He kissed her fingers again. "Besides, this way Molly can stay in school and you can continue to teach if you wish."

"You don't mind if I keep my job?"

"Well, for now, at least. I hope perhaps in the future…" He stopped. Better not talk about babies. She was blushing enough already. "Well, you may teach as long as you like."

He slipped down onto the grass, glad it had dried, although he could still feel damp earth underneath the grass. "Helen, will you marry me?"

Tears pooled in her eyes and she nodded. "Yes, Patrick. I'd be honored to be your wife."

He quickly reclaimed his place beside her and took her into his arms. The first touch of their lips made his head reel. "Helen," he whispered, "can we make it soon?"

Helen gazed up into Patrick's eyes, hardly able to believe she wasn't dreaming. She'd dared to dream about this moment, but the reality was so much more wonderful than her dreams. "How soon do you mean?"

"Of course I want you to have a proper engagement period, and I'll need to get moved and start looking for some land for a house. I wouldn't ask you to live in the rooms over the store."

"I wouldn't mind," she said then wondered again if her words were too bold.

"But I'd mind for you." He peered into her eyes. "I don't even know if you have family to consider."

She shook her head. "My father died when I was thirteen, and my mother passed away five years ago. I was an only child. Do you have family other than Molly?"

"No, what family members I have left are in Ireland."

She reached up and smoothed back the lock of hair that had fallen across his eye. "I love your hair."

He laughed. "You like this carrot-colored thicket?"

"It isn't carrot colored. It's a beautiful deep, dark red and it goes perfectly with your eyes."

"Well, my darling, I only hope our children look like you. That's all I've got to say."

She bit her lip, fighting off embarrassment, then laughed. "I guess that must be a compliment."

"Very much so. You're beautiful, Helen. Don't you know that?" His eyes spoke even more than his words.

"Well, thank you. I'm glad you think so." She thought a minute. "I'll ask Molly to be my bridesmaid."

"She'll love that." His tender look caused butterflies to come alive in her stomach.

"I wouldn't want anyone else."

"Would the end of summer be too soon?" His hopeful look almost persuaded her.

"I'd sort of like an autumn wedding, if you don't mind. It's my favorite time of year." Although Georgia autumns didn't have the lovely colors and crisp days she'd grown up with. Still…the thought of walking down the aisle in a wedding dress in the sweltering heat of a Georgia August was totally unbearable. Imagine if her face should perspire and she couldn't even blot it with a handkerchief.

"Then autumn, it is. You set the date and make the arrangements you like. Don't worry about the expense. I'll take care of it."

"You'll do no such thing," she retorted. "My parents left me with a tidy little dowry of sorts. It will do nicely to pay for the wedding and then some."

He laughed. "Are you always this stubborn?"

She threw him a teasing smile. "Oh no, sometimes I'm much worse. Want to call off the wedding?"

"Not a chance." He grinned. "I like stubborn women."

"Sometimes I'm very easy to get along with." She smiled, wondering what he'd say next. Not really caring, just wanting to hear his voice.

"I know." He tweaked her chin. "I like you that way even better."

The afternoon flew by. Helen felt as though they were the only two people on earth. Then they heard Albert coming up the lane, singing an old gospel hymn.

Helen gasped. "They must be stopping for the day. Have we been out here that long?"

"Doesn't seem that long." Patrick sighed and rose, helping her to her feet. "I think we'd better tell Molly the news before I go, don't you?"

"Of course. You don't think I can keep this secret until next weekend, do you?"

They strolled up the lane hand in hand until Helen gently pulled hers away.

They waited until after supper to tell Molly. They went out on the front porch, and surrounded by the sound of chirping birds and blossom scented air, they told her the news.

"Oh, Papa. Oh, Miss Edwards. I've been praying you'd

fall in love and get married." She took a deep breath. "Does this mean you'll be my mother?"

"Molly," Helen heard her own voice tremble, "I know you had a wonderful mother and I would never try to take her place, but I do want to be a mother to you. If you want me to."

Molly threw her arms around Helen. "I do. I really do." She pulled back and looked up into Helen's face. "Will I still have to call you Miss Edwards?"

Helen gave a shaky little laugh. "Well, you'll have to call me Miss Edwards until the wedding. After that, you'll call me Mrs. Flannigan in school and you can decide what you want to call me at home."

"Can I think about it?"

Patrick gave Molly a hug. "Yes, you have plenty of time to think about it. Do you think you can keep it a secret for a little while? Just until we get a chance to announce it?"

The stricken look on Molly's face told the answer very clearly. "Can't you announce it now? So I can tell Trudy and Margaret?"

Helen glanced at Patrick and met his waiting eyes. He grinned. "I guess there's no getting around it."

Helen laughed. "Let's tell P.J. and Hannah and Charles anyway. Oh, and Howard and Felicity. So they won't hear the news from the children."

They found Hannah and Felicity in the parlor with Virgie and told them the news. Virgie didn't say I told you so, but the smile on her face spoke volumes.

After they'd shared the news with the others, Molly kissed her father good night and went upstairs.

Helen followed Patrick out to the porch. Their tender farewell left Helen in tears.

"Please don't cry, sweetheart. I'll be back soon."

"They're happy tears. I promise. I'll be fine."

She stood there while he went for his horse then watched him ride away. But this time, she knew he'd be coming back, not just to Molly but to her.

Her prayers that night were mingled with laughter and tears. *Thank you, Lord. You've given me my heart's desire.*

Patrick stepped into his new building. The previous owner had left it clean and in good repair. There really wasn't too much he'd need to do to ready it for its transformation into a leather shop. He missed the smell of oiled leather, and his hand, mind, and heart were eager to get back to their trade. Well, his mind and heart were more focused on Helen right now, but he was determined to build the business up. A man couldn't be truly happy unless he provided for his family. And he intended to do just that.

He worked until midnight, getting the existing shelves into the position he wanted them. The glass-doored cabinets were a bonus, since the ones he used for display in the Atlanta shop were built-in. So this was one expense he'd not have.

He went upstairs and took another look at the living quarters. There were three small rooms. He didn't want to crowd Molly and Helen into such a small space, but it would be fine for him while he was looking for a home-place.

The Atlanta house looked small and forlorn with all its furniture and pretty knickknacks sold or packed away. He'd gotten rid of all the furniture. He couldn't expect Helen to live among Maureen's things. He'd already bought a few pieces of furniture for his rooms above the shop and he'd buy more for the new house whenever he had one.

He'd saved some things for Molly, including the clock that had belonged to Maureen's family and the linens and china she'd brought from Ireland. Molly would want those when she was a grown-up woman. Just for a moment the familiar twinge bit at him. But quickly he shoved it aside. His grief was gone. At most, what he'd just felt was nostalgia. Maureen was his first love and always would be. But the love he felt for Helen, though different, was just as strong, perhaps stronger in its own way.

He ran his hand over the mantel he'd built the year they'd arrived here. He spoke, slipping back into the brogue he'd tried so hard to leave behind. "I'll be leavin' ya now, lass. But, I'll be seein' you again someday. And you'll meet Helen, too, and I know you'll be lovin' her. Just you wait and see."

Turning his back on the place where he'd loved and lost Maureen, he shut the door behind him and got on his horse to head for the train station for the last time.

Chapter 19

December 1892

Helen jumped out of bed and hurried to turn the page on the huge calendar that hung behind her washstand. The first day of December. Just two weeks and two days until her wedding day. Butterflies banged against her stomach. She giggled. She did a lot of that lately. But why shouldn't a woman giggle when her wedding approached. Even if she had turned thirty-three last month.

She ran her finger down the calendar. The children would be dismissed for the Christmas break on the sixteenth. She pressed her fingers against her lips and then allowed her fingers to rest on the eighteenth. She was so glad her wedding fell on a Sunday. They planned to have the wedding at the church at two o'clock. She had no idea where they'd spend the night. Patrick said he wanted to surprise her. They'd leave for Savannah the next morn-

ing for a short honeymoon and be back the Friday before
Christmas. Their first Christmas as a family. Molly was
so delighted she didn't mind staying at the school while
they were away. The teachers and other students would
all be gone. But Felicity and Virgie would take good care
of her and Selma had promised to let her help bake cookies and pies for the remaining staff's Christmas holiday.
And of course, Virgie's small grandson would be there a
lot as always.

She did her morning ablutions and got dressed. After
tucking her hair into a bun, she grabbed the stack of graded
essays from her writing desk. She'd take them upstairs to
her classroom before going down to breakfast.

She arrived at the dining room door just as Sissy arrived with a fresh urn of hot coffee. The girl smiled and
motioned with her head for Helen to precede her through
the open doorway.

The buffet was already set with breakfast foods, including Helen's favorites—ham, fried eggs, and grits dripping
in butter. She added a biscuit to her plate for good measure
and sat down. Sissy brought her a cup of coffee.

"Thank you. I could have gotten that."

"Yes, miss." She pressed her lips together then grinned.
"But you already sittin' down and I was up. Anyway, you
goin' be pourin' enough coffee once you is married to
that Irishman."

Friendly laughter rippled across the table. Everyone
seemed to think it was funny that the prim and proper
Helen was marrying the wild-haired Irishman. Well, she'd
show them.

"Actually, Sissy, I thought I'd turn all the domestic duties over to Patrick."

This time, after a shocked instance of silence, uproarious laughter burst out, followed by Molly's dismayed voice. "You mean Papa is going to do the cooking?"

Uh oh, she may have gone too far. "No, of course not, Molly. I was only teasing. I promise I'll cook and clean and do laundry."

Molly blew a breath of air out. "Oh, good, but you won't have to clean or do laundry. Papa is going to hire a maid." She clapped a hand over his mouth. "Oh no. That was supposed to be a surprise."

"Don't worry, I won't let on that I know." Helen glanced around the room and placed a finger to her lips. "No one else will tell, either."

That wasn't the only secret. Patrick had found them land with a small but nicely built house already on it. He'd been working on it for the last three months, and Helen hadn't been allowed to see whatever improvements he'd made. She had a sneaky hunch he might be adding a room but wasn't sure. Ordinarily, curiosity would be getting intense, but with the excitement of planning for the wedding and the birth of Abigail's baby daughter, there hadn't been a lot of time to dwell on it.

Baby Celeste had been born in early October and had quickly stolen everyone's heart. Abigail looked nearly as trim as she had at her wedding. She had agreed to be Helen's matron of honor.

After breakfast, Helen went to her classroom. Within a few minutes her first hour students filed in.

Lily Ann took her desk near the front, so Helen could help her with braille in between her other teaching duties. Abigail had decided not to return to teaching and Helen didn't blame her. P.J. was looking for a braille instructor since they were expecting two more blind students the following year, including an eleven-year-old deaf-blind boy.

The thought of living with a double handicap like that

was overwhelming to Helen, and she had no idea how anyone could teach him. But on the other hand, who would have thought a blind child like Lily Ann could have learned sign language, which she insisted on doing? The deaf children signed in her hand or finger spelled and it worked quite well. It had opened more communication between Lily Ann and the other children. But of course, Lily Ann also had her hearing.

A ripple of excitement ran through her at the thought of helping more students. Of course, if she and Patrick had children of their own, she would need to retire from teaching, at least until they were older.

"Miss Edwards!" Phoebe's broken speech brought her back to the present. She was having a little trouble focusing today.

"Yes, Phoebe?" She stepped over to the child's desk.

"Bobby and Sonny keep pulling my hair." She was nearly in tears.

Helen glanced at Bobby, who sat behind Phoebe, and Sonny, who sat beside Bobby. Both had guilty but gleeful looks on their faces. She motioned for them both to follow her and led them out the door and into the hallway.

"All right, boys." She spoke while she signed. The little rascals wouldn't be able to say they didn't hear her. They were both proficient in sign and lip reading. "I know those long blond braids are tempting to pull. It's probably a lot of fun."

They both gave vigorous nods.

"But did it ever cross your minds that those braids are attached to Phoebe's scalp and it hurts when you yank on them?"

They looked at each other then looked away.

Bobby spoke first. "I didn't think about that. I won't do it anymore, Miss Edwards. I promise."

"I won't, either." Sonny made a crossing motion in the general vicinity of his heart.

"I think you need to both apologize to Phoebe."

Dread crossed their faces.

"In front of everbody?" Bobby's eyes widened.

"Right now would be a good time." She tapped her foot and gave them a stern look.

"Yes, ma'am," they chorused.

The boys shuffled into the classroom and marched back to Phoebe's desk. After apologizing, they took their seats.

"Do you forgive them, Phoebe?" Helen asked the frowning little girl.

"Yes, I forgive them." The frown lines became deeper. "But aren't they going to get a whipping?"

Helen bit her lip. Apparently Phoebe needed a little teaching on forgiveness.

"I don't think that's necessary." She tossed a warning glance at both boys. "But if they ever do it again, they'll go to the director's office and I don't know what Miss Wellington might decide to do."

Helen returned to her seat, hoping the rest of the day would be uneventful. She couldn't wait until supper time. Patrick would be here.

Patrick stood back and surveyed the house. He hoped Helen would love it as much as he did. He'd finally had to face the fact that he wasn't a good enough carpenter to do what he wanted and get it done in time, especially since he also had to run his business. So he'd hired several carpenters to do most of the work for him

A wide porch stretched across the front of the whit frame house wrapping around one side where it met L from the added room. There was plenty of space more rooms if they needed them. Or they could a second floor. But for now, he thought it was just about perfect.

He'd already brought in the furniture he and Helen had picked out. And he'd placed the heirloom clock on the mantel in Molly's room. He'd let her decide which of Maureen's other things she wanted to display. He hoped she'd keep them in the cedar chest at the end of her bed until her own wedding.

He mounted the midnight-black gelding he'd recently purchased. The new carriage and two carriage horses were housed in the barn along with a milk cow. It was a hassle to come out here twice a day to take care of the livestock, but he had found some very good deals which he hadn't wanted to pass up.

He rode into town and went to his rooms above the shop. His employee, Jim Porter, would move in there this weekend, when Patrick planned to take up residence in the new house.

He changed and headed for the school. He couldn't wait to see Helen and Molly. Soon, they'd all be together—a family in their own home.

Helen couldn't breathe. She gasped. Panic took over and she looked around wildly.

Abigail gave her a worried look. "Be still and breathe in slowly, then let it out slowly. Now do it again. That's good. You're fine. Just a case of nerves."

Helen concentrated on slow breathing while Abigail adjusted her veil, drawing it down over her face. "You didn't fall apart at your wedding."

Abigail laughed. "That's what you think. But I had my mother there and that helped. Just pretend I'm your mother."

Helen giggled. "How can I pretend that? You're five years younger than I am.

"There, you have your laughter back. You'll be fine. Especially when you start down the aisle and see Patrick looking at you all gooey eyed."

"Gooey eyed?" Helen wailed. "Now I'm going to think of that when I look at him. If I start laughing while walking down the aisle, you're a dead goose."

"I promise you won't think about anything but Patrick." She patted the veil. "There, you're ready. And I hear the music. We need to go to the door to the vestibule so we can see Molly walk in."

They peeked in and watched Molly step through the door to the sanctuary. She walked down the aisle in perfect step to the music. Abigail patted Helen on the shoulder and stepped away.

She took a deep breath. She wondered how long it would take Abigail to walk down the aisle.

The music got louder and she heard her cue. She stepped on the red carpet and started down the aisle. Lifting her eyes, she looked toward the front of the church. The reverend was at the front and Dr. Trent stood by Patrick's side. As she looked directly at Patrick, her heart almost stopped. The expression on his face showed adoration and eternal love. She was about to be joined to her dream man. No, better than that. The godly man the Lord had brought into her life. He stepped forward and took her hand. She felt numb and yet tingling with life at the same time. She heard the reading of the vows. She heard herself answer and then Patrick.

Then loudly and clearly the reverend said, "I now pronounce you man and wife. You may kiss the bride."

Patrick gently lifted her veil and bent his lips to hers and she melted into his embrace.

A roar of noise brought her back to reality as their friends clapped.

The reception didn't last long and soon Helen was kissing Molly. "Sweetie, we'll see you in a few days. I'll miss you."

"I'll miss you, too, Mama."

Electricity ran down Helen's entire body. Molly had called her *mama*. She winked back tears and hugged Molly tightly. "I love you, Molly."

Then she was swept past the crowd and into the carriage. She leaned her head on Patrick's shoulder as they drove away.

Patrick slipped his arm around her. "I love you, Mrs. Flannigan."

"Oh. I love that name. And I love you, Mr. Flannigan." She looked up into his eyes. "Where are we going?"

"We're almost there. Close your eyes."

She laughed as joy came flooding up. "Oh, all right." She shut her eyes tightly.

The carriage turned and a few minutes later, stopped.

"You can open your eyes now."

Her lashes fluttered up and she looked at their house. But was it the same house? It was magnificent. She drew her breath in. "Oh, Patrick. It's beautiful. I love our new home. The porch is wonderful."

He hopped out and came around to lift her down. Instead of putting her on the ground he carried her up the porch steps and opened the door. Her heart thumped as he carried her over the threshold of their home.

When he set her on her feet, she swayed, and he caught her, drawing her closely to him. He pressed his lips to hers, gently at first, then deeper. "Welcome home, Helen."

"Oh, Patrick, my darling. I was home the moment we

were pronounced man and wife. But here, in this wonderful place, we can start our life together."

And then his lips claimed hers again.

* * * * *

REQUEST YOUR FREE BOOKS!

2 FREE CHRISTIAN NOVELS
PLUS 2
FREE
MYSTERY GIFTS

HEARTSONG
PRESENTS

REQUEST YOUR FREE BOOKS!

2 FREE INSPIRATIONAL NOVELS
PLUS 2
FREE
MYSTERY GIFTS

Love Inspired®

LIDIR12